Leptis Magna

Emperor's Dream on the Edge of the Desert

Book 1: Leptis Magna

Book 2: Court of the Soldier Emperor

Book 3: Memoirs of a Bishop

A search for meaning and redemption as one world passes and another emerges

Michael Hugos

(email: mhugos@yahoo.com)

Book 1 photo:
David Gunn, 2006
Severan Arch, Leptis Magna, Libya
Wikimedia Commons

Book 2 photo:
Colossus of Barletta, 4th Century
Emperor Valentinian
Wikimedia Commons

Book 3 photo:
Courtesy of Coptic Museum, Cairo
Mural painting, Late Roman Period
The Monastery of Saint Jeremiah at Saqqara, Egypt

****

Revised edition with maps
10 October 2016

To Venetia in movement and repose

Table of Contents

Leptis Magna

Emperor's Dream on the Edge of the Desert

BOOK 1

Chapter 1

The Later Roman Empire

I was born in the days when the Emperor Constantine and his heirs took the empire in their firm grasp and strove mightily to restore our past glory. In truth that restoration was only for some and not for all, yet it seemed for a while that the many pieces of empire could indeed be put back together again. But in attempting to recreate what once was, we have done much to destroy what still remains.

And I have been part of that destruction. I did not intend to do what I did. I am a good man, and yet I am far from blameless.

How could I have done this? I claimed it was for the good of the city and my family and all the traditions that make us who we are. And now I search for a way to live with myself.

Often I wake in the middle of the night after only a few hours sleep. I get out of bed and put on my robe, I light my lamp, and make my way through the darkened house. Down the long hallway, past empty rooms and up flights of stairs to my study, to my library of manuscripts and memories.

As I open the shutters that cover the windows, I see a full moon riding above the city, bathing whitewashed houses and marble clad buildings in a soft glow of ghostly light. I hear the sound of waves, and I smell the sea, just a short walk down the street from my front door.

My library is on the third floor at the back of the family house. Looking out the window on one side I see the streets and buildings that lead to the old forum down by the harbor with its ancient temples and old city senate house. Through the other window I see the high city walls of Leptis Magna just a few blocks away. On the other side of the walls are the abandoned districts that the walls could not enclose. Drifting sand covers over what remains of the buildings and buries the streets. Desert is reclaiming land no longer shaded by trees, no longer tended by farmers. This is not the city I remember.

I place the candles and olive oil lamps in my library to create a circle of light, and in this light, and on this night, I am once again consumed by the task of understanding what happened, and why, and what it means.

Shelves packed with books and scrolls cover the walls behind me. My big wooden table and cushioned chair sit in the middle of the room allowing me to look up from my work and see the city and the sea. From a shelf where I keep my latest work I pull out my manuscript and open it on my writing table. I dip my quill in a pot of ink, and continue again where I left off the night before.

In My Time

My name is Septimius Lucius, and I write these words in the autumn of the year 384 AD in the province of Tripolitania, in the reign of the Emperor Valentinian II. Here in my study in the small hours of the night, I turn to my writing in an attempt to connect who I was with who I am, to retrace my steps, to understand the sequence of events that brought me here. As I recount one story, it brings forth others. I write them down and piece them together in combinations that might possibly explain how the past became the present.

These stories are true. The names and dates and events I recount here are accurate to the best of my ability. Works of the historians will bear me out for those who consult their books to verify my facts. Yet although the facts and events are true, what still remains unclear is the meaning of these events, and whether they could have happened some other way.

To be honest with myself, as I must, these stories show that what I did, and what a brave man should do, were two quite different things. Any thoughtful reader can see through the reasons I offer, and in any case, those reasons are no excuse for the consequences that followed. Yet I continue with this writing because I must find a way to relieve myself of this terrible regret. I must find some plausible explanation that exonerates me, and lets me slip away from my burden of shame.

Instead of being a means for escape, this writing has become a confession of my guilt. Yet in this city now there is no one to whom I can make my confession, no one except myself. I am both bishop and chief magistrate. "*Pater, peccavi, ignosce mi.*" Father, I have sinned, forgive me.

I relied on reason alone. I did not know or chose not to see that when reason comes up against emotion unrestrained by discipline, then reason alone cannot prevail. Even now as I write these words, I feel again those emotions; those primal emotions that swept us away in the panic that seized our city. Why did I not have the courage then to save me from this fate today?

In that panic only one man stood to defend us, and that man was not me. Though it was my place and my honor to stand at his side, I did not. And in the flood of events that followed, much was lost.

The years since have shown ever so clearly that what I bought in that time of panic was only a slow death instead of a quick one. I paid for this purchase with my self-respect. Next week I return to Alexandria. I find it a struggle to continue.

But enough of my confessions for the moment… let me rise above the moment and paint a larger picture. This picture emerges in fragments as I write my stories and arrange them like pieces of a mosaic to show what happened. As the picture becomes clearer, perhaps it will help me understand why these events occurred as they did, and help me see if they could have, somehow, happened differently.

Let me start at the beginning.

The Villa Selene

I was born in 341, and my earliest memories are of growing up at our estate in the country outside of Leptis. My family had a villa on the coast. It was called the Villa Selene. Selene was the goddess of the Moon. She held sway over the night and the tides. And all those elements came together to imprint themselves deeply on my memory from earliest childhood. The sound of waves washing up on the beach and the sparkle of moonlight reflecting off the water combine with memories of cool breezes blowing though my sleeping room in the summer time, bringing with them the smell of the sea.

In the entrance way as one entered our villa the wall was covered with a mosaic commissioned by my great grandfather. It showed Aion the god of eternity holding a hoop and through that hoop passed a procession of the four seasons, Winter, Spring, Summer and Autumn. Each season had her child with her. I always identified myself as Summer's child because that child had my dark hair and he seemed to be pulling away from his mother and looking off at some other place where he wanted to be.

Aion was seated and turned at the waist as he held his hoop of eternity. Standing next to him with her hand on his shoulder was Venus. I always thought of them as my mother and father. The two of them were a well matched couple; so sure of themselves and the rightness of their beliefs. I thought they would live forever.

My mother and father expected us to grow up and follow in their footsteps, and live the life and perform the duties that sons and daughters from a family such as ours are expected to perform. We were those children in the mosaic being led through endless cycles of time by the four seasons. This was our duty and our destiny.

Our villa sat on a small promontory rising up from long sandy beaches on either side. The floor plan was like the letter H. There were two straight wings on either side of a peristyle garden and a connecting hall between them that closed off the garden on the landward side. The seaward side of the garden was open leading onto a wide terrace with staircases going down to the beach on either side.

The wing on the western side of the house contained my parents' sleeping room, and in a spacious room at the end, facing the sea, was my father's library. Shelves of scrolls and books lined two of the walls; windows looking out on the sea took much of the other two walls. A door from his library opened onto the colonnaded terrace that surrounded the garden on three sides and shaded our house in the heat of the day. On the other side of the house the eastern wing contained our sleeping rooms. Beyond the sleeping rooms, the eastern wing connected to a bath complex my grandfather had built many years ago. It was complete with steam rooms where we went to relax and sweat and servants would rub us down with olive oil and gently scrape away the dirt of the day, and wrap us in robes to take a nap before dinner.

Depending on the season, we took our meals either in the summer dining room or the winter dining room. The summer dining room was in the part of the house that connected the two wings. A wide door opened directly onto the garden, and there was a view of the peristyle garden and the ocean beyond. It was said our dinning room had the most perfect view to be found. In the winter we ate in the dining room on the west side of the house where it was warmed in the afternoon by the low hanging sun in the western sky at that time of year.

I am overwhelmed by these memories of what seemed like paradise. Timeless rhythms marked by the sound of the waves and the passing of the seasons. The predictable patterns of activity; the pruning of vines and olive trees in the late winter; the planting of wheat and barley as the spring progressed; the tending of animals and the first vegetable harvests of the summer; leading to the long and sometimes frantic days in the early autumn when the harvest was the center of everyone's attention.

After the harvest was in, there were festivals and the pressing of the olives for their oil and the crushing of the grapes for their juice. And then the winter came. It was cold and overcast and rainy, and we stayed indoors where our tutors taught us grammar and mathematics. We learned to read, and recited passages from the heroic tales of Homer and Virgil.

One day when my father came back from a trip to Carthage he presented my mother with a gift. The gift was a fair skinned servant girl he had bought in the slave market there. Mother had servants, but she still spent much of her day watching over us and worrying about what trouble we might get into. There were four of us children, me the oldest at eight and my younger brothers and sister. We were a handful. Father bought her someone to look after us and keep us out of trouble.

Her name was Uta. She was born a barbarian in the northern forests on the far side of the Rhine River. She and many of her people were captured in one of the campaigns our legions fought periodically to pacify those people and punish them for raiding the Roman towns and farms on our side of the river. Young female slaves were always in demand, and she was taken and trained as a house servant. Now she was 17 or 18 years old and my father had paid a fine price for her I am sure.

That summer afternoon when Mother introduced her to us I was immediately taken by the calm self-possessed way she greeted us. Mother called out our names one at a time, and each time she called one of our names, Uta made eye contact, then curtsied and smiled. Mother made it clear that when she was not around, we were to listen to Uta and do as she said, or our father would hear about our misbehavior.

Uta became quite protective of my youngest brother and sister and would not let me or my other brother tease them. She could get quite cross and even confrontational when she wanted to or when we ignored her and pretended we didn't hear her. I soon sensed that she expected me to set the example for my brothers and sister to follow. She did this in many subtle ways. She often looked at me first when speaking to all of us. Or she called me by name in front of the others when she gave instructions. She also served me first as a sign of respect I thought, on those afternoons when we came in from swimming or exploring, or when we finished some lesson that our tutor had given us. She made me feel like the man of the house when my father was not around.

I am a Libyan and a Roman of a senatorial family. This pale northern woman with light golden hair and blue eyes was not the image of any woman I expected to marry, and she could never be more than a servant in our house. And yet in those days of growing up; in those years before puberty strikes and utterly confuses the minds of young men, I was captivated by Uta. Her approval was in some ways more important than the approval of my own parents. She spoke from her barbarian culture and yet presented a notion of honor and duty that any Roman of my class feels is part of his destiny. She spoke not so much in words but in eye contact that made me stop what I was doing for a moment. From her, a nod of the head, a smile, and her simple, direct gaze ignited a warm glow in my chest.

One summer morning I woke early. There had been a driving rainstorm the night before accompanied by much lightning and thunder. The storm had passed and it was quiet and sunny that morning but the waves were still high, reflecting the night just passed. Waves rolled in toward the beach, and as they did, they swelled up and curled over and came crashing down on the sand.

I walked out of my sleeping room and stood on the terrace watching the waves. Nobody else was up as far as I could tell. Then I turned and there was Uta. She smiled and motioned me to follow her as she headed for the steps from the terrace that led down to the beach. I stood there. She looked back and motioned me again. I ran to catch up.

I was still in my sleeping clothes, a loose shirt and short baggy pants. She was dressed to go for an early morning swim; her breasts where bound almost flat with a wide band of cloth around her chest and she wore loose fitting pants tied securely around her hips. She stepped onto the sand and looked back and then ran down the beach toward the waves.

We started running along the beach, and charging into the waves as they crashed down on the sand. I suddenly understood, Uta was treating me as a playmate or a friend. That simple, direct smiling face of hers was focused on me as her companion. I was elated. She followed my lead as I ran off in search of more big waves. She caught up with me and we laughed as we ran. Another big wave approached, and we ran into it and emerged from the foaming water laughing. We swung each other around and ran into another big foaming wave.

Then we saw an approaching wave that was the biggest one yet. We looked at each other and raced to see who would be the first to plunge into this one. Uta was first and I followed right after. This one pushed me down onto my knees on the hard sand as it came crashing down on top of me. I ran out of the water back up onto the dry sand. When I turned around and looked back, I saw Uta come running out of the water toward me. The wave had pushed the band of cloth around her breasts down to her waist.

I saw firm pale breasts with brown nipples sticking out like small thumbs. What can a young boy already in love with an older woman do but stare? She was laughing and running toward me and then she must have seen the expression on my face. I thought she and her pale breasts and her strong thighs and her wet golden hair were a vision of the goddess Selene herself. In that moment Uta was the object of my rapt attention and utter devotion.

She laughed and looked at me, and pulled up the cloth and tied it around her breasts again. Then she said we should go back to the house and see if my brothers or sister were up and bring them down to the beach with us. We did that. And as we all walked from the house back to the beach I told one of my brothers about how Uta's top had come down and how I had seen her breasts. For the next hour Uta led us on charge after charge into the big waves. And we two boys hoped each time that the next big wave would do its magic and reveal again a vision of those beautiful breasts. It did not happen; we were very disappointed. Yet needless to say, I have never forgotten the vision of Uta on the beach that morning.

Uta became the personification of summer for me. Summer for me is warm and golden with firm breasts and a smile I cannot resist. As the years went by Uta merged in my mind with the goddess of summer portrayed in the mosaic of the four seasons passing through the hoop of eternity in the entryway of our villa.

A Story Told by a Woman

I think history is a story told by a woman. I think this because the best history is made of stories that are more than dates and battles and names of generals and kings. Those straight, rational recordings of events are helpful, yet lacking in subtle details to understand what motivated the people. Official histories often assign convenient reasons to events, yet lack convincing evidence to show those reasons are true.

It is the women in my family who are keepers of the stories. It seems they are more attuned to the subtleties and emotions that drive us. Those subtleties and emotions once sounded to me like so much noise and gossip. But upon closer listening over the years, it is in those subtleties that I hear the timeless truths and glimpse the wisdom I seek.

Stories that fill in the straight and rational recordings with telling details of personalities and desires; those are the stories that make history speak. It is history such as that which offers lessons and suggests how I might apply those lessons to my present predicament. Just as the Muse is a woman, I am certain History too is a woman.

History is a story told by a woman
Because it goes on and on, rich in detail
With characters whose lives engage and seduce me.

Tell me stories of people and what they did
Tell me - am I of them?
Or for them?
Or against them?

What did they do right, what did they do wrong?
Your stories of courage give me courage
Your stories of greatness give me guidance.

I fall into your stories as I fall into your eyes,
Seeking your wisdom, seeking to find myself in your grace
Looking for eternity by merging my life in yours.

Imperious and Imperial Ancestor

There are stories in our family that are passed from one generation to the next. These stories tell us who we are and how we came to be. Many of them, maybe even most of them, seem to start with or relate in some way to our most famous ancestor, Lucius Septimius Severus. He was known by his cognomen – Severus.

When the Praetorians murdered the Emperor Pertinax, Severus marched his Pannonian legions to Rome to avenge that crime. His coins had his image on one side and on the other was a winged Victory holding a palm frond and the motto "Vic Pan" to commemorate the victory of his Pannonian legions. Because of that victory he became emperor. Severus was my great, great, great, great granduncle.

Lucius Septimius Severus became emperor in the year 195. And when that happened, this city, our city, became an imperial city because it was the place he was born and raised. He was the native son who became ruler of the Romans. He was an African, a Phoenician, a Berber, but not an Italian. He was Libyan. He spoke Punic first and learned Latin in school.

One story has it that Severus early on believed he was destined to be the imperator – the general who becomes emperor. We were already a senatorial family and maintained a suitably stylish villa just outside Rome where members of the family lived and entertained on a lavish scale. One such event was a small dinner held for a visiting nephew of the emperor Marcus Aurelius. Severus had just arrived in Rome so he was not known to the servants of the house. As he arrived at the villa on that evening of the dinner, the servants mistook him for the nephew of the emperor and showed him to the seat of honor which was draped with a purple cloak. Severus said nothing and accepted the seat as if it was his rightful place. All turned to look, and no one said a word.

The real imperial nephew had not yet arrived and Severus was in no hurry to move. He calmly turned his head to look at each family member in the room. He looked them each straight in the eye. And only then, did he get up slowly, and move to a different seat being held for him by a nervous servant.

We had significant business interests related to the importing of African olive oil and wheat to supply the dole for feeding the population of Rome. We and other prominent families of Leptis had connections, and sons were already following their fathers into promising careers in the imperial service. The emperor Hadrian acknowledged this when he endowed our city with the imposing limestone and marble building that houses the city's public baths and exercise grounds. Even today this building dominates that part of the city with its presence. It was a sign of imperial Roman respect.

Severus was taught by teachers in Leptis and Carthage. Soon after his eighteenth birthday he went to Rome where Emperor Marcus Aurelius made him a senator. And he then began an assent through positions of increasing responsibility in the civil service and the military. In 191 the emperor Commodus appointed him governor of Upper Pannonia and commander of the two legions stationed there to guard the frontier along the Danube River.

Four years later Commodus died under unusual circumstances, and the senate elected one of their own, Pertinax, to be the next emperor. But after only a few months the Praetorian Guards objected to some of the policies he proclaimed, and they murdered him. The Praetorians then proceeded to auction off the emperor's title to the highest bidder. The winner of that auction, a silly fool of a rich banker, Didus Julianus, sent cart loads of money and gold to the camp of the Praetorians just outside Rome. He then enjoyed the absurd experience of acting as if he was the emperor for six months. How could he possibly have thought anyone would take him seriously? He was merely the Praetorians' pet poodle. As it turned out, they offered him up quickly enough when it came time to save their own skins.

Upon hearing of the murder of Pertinax, and then the selling of the emperor's title, Severus proclaimed it his duty to avenge these crimes and restore the dignity of the empire. He was also the general whose legions were closest to Rome.

As he marched his troops toward Rome, he sent messengers ahead to communicate his wishes and intentions. His first wish was for the Praetorians to hand over the puppet to whom they had sold the title of emperor. Upon hearing of this request, that poor puppet disguised himself as a servant and attempted to escape from the palace and slip out of Rome. He was caught, executed, and his body was sent to Severus.

As Severus came on toward Rome, the Praetorians grew increasingly anxious. And they had good reason to be. Severus sent a succession of messengers to communicate his disapproval of what they had done. Finally, as he neared the city, he ordered the Praetorians to come out to meet him. He ordered them to come without arms or armor. They did so knowing they had no choice, for if they resisted they would certainly be killed. They were no match for the battle hardened soldiers who marched with Severus.

Out they came from Rome to meet Severus and his legions. The Praetorians drew themselves up in formation in a field next to the highway called the Via Flaminia and waited. As Severus approached, he encircled them with his own soldiers in full battle dress with swords drawn. The Praetorians were terrified. They knelt in the field and pleaded for mercy. They quickly handed over those who ordered the assassination of Emperor Pertinax and those who actually carried out the deed. Those unlucky Praetorians were executed on the spot.

Then Severus stepped forward and addressed the rest. He said he would show them his mercy and let them live. However, he went on, they and their Praetorian Guard were disbanded for their treachery, and they were all banished, never again to set foot in the city of Rome.

Then he marched on and entered the city with his legions. The Senate turned out with the rest of the population to welcome him. There, in front of the Senate and the people of Rome, "Senatus Populusque Romanus – SPQR," as it is said, and with his soldiers looking on, Severus proclaimed himself emperor.

All hailed the conquering hero.

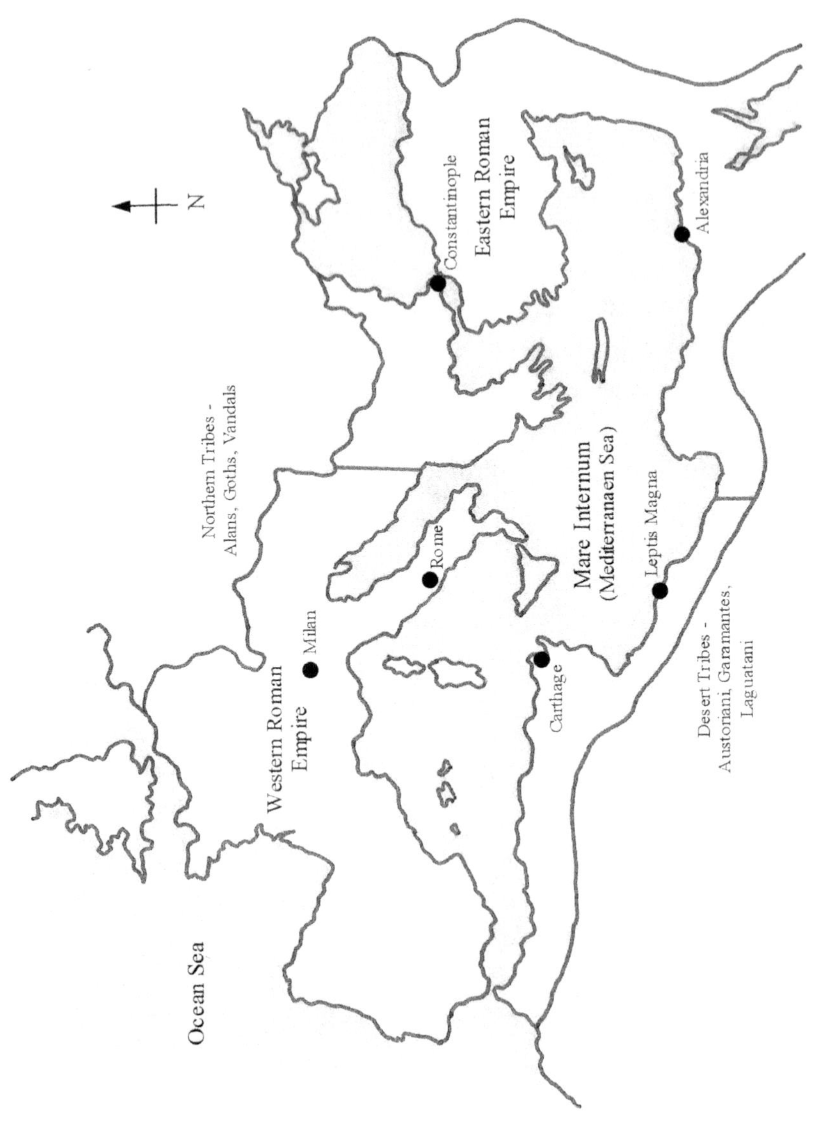
N
Northern Tribes -
Alans, Goths, Vandals
Constantinople
Eastern Roman
Empire
Alexandria
Ocean Sea
Western Roman
Empire
Milan
Rome
Mare Internum
(Mediterranaen Sea)
Leptis Magna
Carthage
Desert Tribes -
Austoriani, Garamantes,
Laguatani

Chapter 2

Nostrae Civitatis

When Severus became emperor our city was already large and prosperous, now he embarked on a building program to endow the city with all the grandeur appropriate to a city that was home to the family of a Roman emperor. He commissioned the best architects to design and build a new monumental core for the city. He would put Leptis Magna on a par with Carthage and even echo some aspects of Rome itself. A ten year building campaign ensued, and when it was finished the effect was stunning. Our city was a vision of opulence in the bright North African sunlight.

Architects from Rome and Athens and Damascus came to Leptis. They presented plans for creating the monumental city the emperor wanted. Land in the middle of the city was cleared of the shops and tenements it once held, and great construction projects began. The city was rebuilt in a style and on a scale befitting the imperial dignity.

Thousands of construction slaves worked from dawn to dusk year after year. Thousands of blocks of finished limestone where carved and carried from a quarry a short distance down the coast. Derricks and cranes were built and powered by gangs of slaves who spent their days walking in tread wheels that operated ropes and gears and winches to move and lift into place the heavy limestone blocks, and the bricks and cement and wood and metal and marble needed to construct this grand new city. They say slaves tired and died by the hundreds on those projects. But Severus kept the army busy with frequent campaigns, and there were always more slaves from conquered enemies to replace those that died.

As I grew old enough to learn more than basic reading, grammar and mathematics, I began spending more time in the city. In my twelfth year I moved into the house of my uncle Jovinus in a fashionable district just west of the theater, close to the sea shore. It was there and in classes taught by philosophers in the forum, that I continued my education.

I began my studies with a Greek teacher who taught me and a group of other boys from other noble families. Each day we met in the forum built by my famous ancestor, the Severan Forum. We learned to recite long passages from the works of Homer and Virgil, Ovid and Cicero. So many references and analogies and phrases of speech come from the works of those authors. It is a rite of indoctrination to learn their fine phrases and use them to construct arguments for or against some course of action or some person. We learned to use those classics to appeal to people's sense of honor, outrage, justice and fairness. All aspiring young men of good families use these skills of rhetoric to advance in their careers.

After classes, wandering back home to my uncle's house, I saw buildings and monuments and fountains everywhere in the city had plaques and inscriptions dedicated to the benefactors who provided the money to build them. Reading these inscriptions and seeing the names of the benefactors, I learned about the history of the city and understood who its important families were then. Much has happened since these buildings were built yet the stones and monuments speak to us and connect us with the people who came before. Severus left many impressive buildings and powerful inscriptions. He impressed himself on our lives for generations to come.

Well before Severus, wealthy patrons had endowed the city with useful and impressive buildings. An inscription next to the main entrance to the city market tells us that in the year 8 BC Annobal Tapapius Rufus bequeathed our city the buildings and precinct of this market which remains in busy use today. The theater near my uncle's house bears an inscription above the main entrance that is written in both Latin and Punic telling us that in the year 2 AD Annobal Rufus provided the money to build the theater. An inscription on a public fountain I often pass on my way announces that in 119 Q. Servilius Candidus financed the building of the aqueduct that brought running water to Leptis all the way from the Cinyps River some 12 miles distant. And the inscription on the Baths says that in 126, the Emperor Hadrian endowed our city with this building as a sign of his favor.

In these inscriptions over the centuries I saw families took Roman names for their sons and daughters, but often kept ancestral Punic names as well. The roots of my own family are Punic. It is said we started with the founding of Leptis some 800 years ago when a Phoenician merchant prince from Tyre married the daughter of a powerful chief of a Berber tribe. Inscriptions in Leptis were commonly in both Latin and Punic until almost the time of Severus. By that time, at the height of the empire, our family and many other good families of Leptis were quick to emphasize their Latin titles and downplay their Punic roots. We were, after all, all Romans.

The Forum of Severus

In the year 198 six blocks of buildings in the middle of the city were demolished and cleared to make room for the new Forum of Severus. It was modeled on the Forum of Trajan in Rome. A rectangular plaza was laid out and surrounded by a tall, marble clad wall of limestone and poured concrete. A two-storey colonnade looked out on three sides of the plaza providing shelter from the sun and rain and spaces for people to meet, for lawyers and merchants to do business, and for teachers to conduct their open air classes with groups of students entrusted to their instruction.

On the side of the forum not enclosed by the colonnade, a temple was built in the classical style with an inner sanctuary surrounded on the outside by tall pillars holding up a massive peaked roof. The temple sits on a podium that elevates it above the forum plaza. This temple was then and is still dedicated to the Severan family.

Across from the temple, on the opposite side of the plaza, is the Severan Basilica. It runs the length of the forum on that side. Its upper story and roof stand above the forum walls and the surrounding buildings and apartment blocks. The main entrance to the basilica is shaded by the colonnade of the forum and framed with richly carved marble and imposing statues.

You can emerge from the Severan temple at one end of the forum, walk down the temple steps, proceed straight across the forum plaza, and enter the center of the basilica through its ornate doorway. Because the colonnade keeps out the direct rays of the sun, inside the basilica is cooler and darker than the heat and bright sunshine outside. The central hall running the length of the basilica has a half-dome apse at each end where judges sit to hear court cases and magistrates set up their tables to conduct the business of the city. On either side of the main hall a row of columns supports a second story gallery running the length of the basilica. Columns on this second story in turn support the ceiling and the roof of the building. All great cities have a basilica like this to house their affairs.

Evening Promenade

The east side of the forum has entrances that open onto a colonnaded avenue that connects the harbor at one end with Hadrian's Baths at the other end. This is the grand promenade of the city. In the evenings after the heat of the day has passed, the avenue is filled with people strolling up from the harbor and down from the Baths and stopping along the way to purchase something to eat or drink from the many small shops that face on the avenue along the length of the forum.

If you turn left upon leaving the forum, you see the harbor and the multi-storied lighthouse of the city perfectly framed by the colonnade on either side of the avenue. If you turn right, you see the Baths and the wide piazza at the head of the avenue. The piazza is bordered on one side by the public gardens in front of the Baths, and on the other side by the two story nymphaeum with its columns and statues of nymphs and gods set into the statue niches lining each story. Its walls form a wide semi-circle of enclosed space and at its base is a pool of water animated by two fountains that gush up in the middle of the pool. The sight and sound of the water is soothing; a cool mist arises from the spray of the fountains.

As I grew into my adolescent years, I turned often to the right upon leaving the forum after classes. The piazza at the head of the avenue was a place where all manner of people mingled. It was a place to go in the evening after spending an afternoon at the Baths. It was a place to see and be seen after business was finished in the forum and the basilica. It was a place where visitors to Leptis and sailors from the ships in the harbor came to marvel at the sights of the city. It was also a place where narrow streets led off into blocks of three and four story tenement buildings. On some of some of those buildings could be seen, carved into their cornerstones, the sign of the erect phallus.

I remember in my fourteenth or fifteenth year how the fire began to burn in my belly. How erections came on at the slightest suggestions or the barest thoughts of certain things. Walking home in the evening along those narrow streets leading off the piazza took me past doorways where women looked at me with meaningful glances and suggestive smiles.

These were the first times in my young life that I came face to face with the contest between reason and emotion, discipline and desire. Prior to this, honor had seemed a clear enough matter of simply choosing the right path and having the good sense to stay on that path.

The houses I passed performed a legal service; they were licensed and taxed by the city. And yet men of good families did not let themselves become the servants of their desires. Another year passed and my honor was in doubt. My reason was shredded by firestorms of desire. My right hand became my best friend and my last refuge before surrender.

I began to notice a certain woman whose door I often passed. When I caught her attention she smiled and made eye contact with me. She had curly black hair to her shoulders, rich brown skin, dark eyes and full lips. She was not the prettiest girl I passed on my walks home in the evening, but the prettiest girls knew they were the prettiest girls, and there was something hard about them that scared me. This woman knew who I was and I fancied she even liked me. I liked her, what little of her I could know. She made me blush when she looked at me. I would smile at her and hurry along the street.

Toward the end of the summer that year, I was coming home with one of my classmates from the forum. As we came up the avenue we met three other classmates standing in the cool air next to the nymphaeum fountain pool. What shall we do? Shall we go to the baths? Shall we walk back down to the harbor and watch the goings on? I forget what I said, but I made my excuses and walked off across the piazza.

The endless chatter in my head was quiet. I knew where I was going without thinking about it. As I walked down the street from the piazza I felt a cool breeze that made me shiver once or twice. I came to her door and looked inside. She looked up and smiled. I walked inside and she took me by the hand and led me down a hallway and into a room off a small garden. She lit a piece of frankincense in an incense burner next to her bed.

She stripped off my clothes and brought me to a washbasin in a corner of the room. She dipped a cloth into the warm water and gently but firmly washed my now erect penis. She took me to her bed and stripped off her simple dress. I beheld curving thighs, beautiful breasts and her pretty face. She looked me in the eyes and smiled.

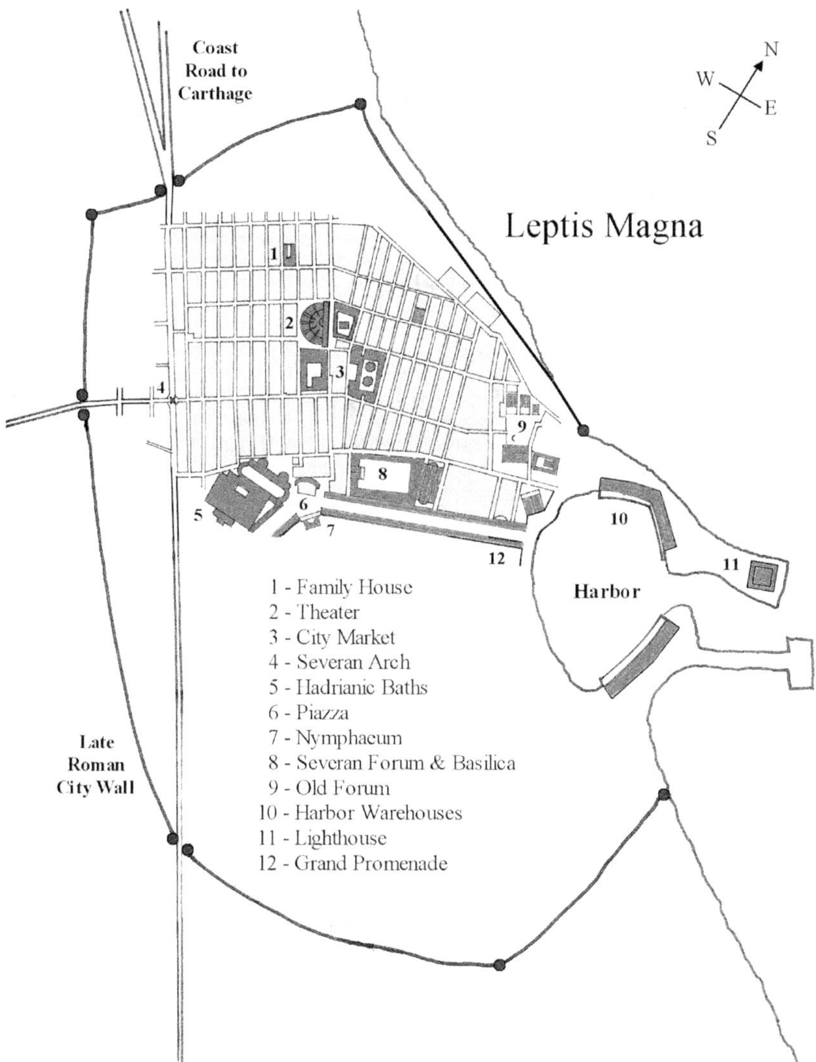

Connection to the World

My uncle Jovinus was the patriarch of our family. He was my father's older brother, and he was the one who people came to see when they wished to do business. It was he who ultimately ran most of the family operations. In addition to our estates, we also owned warehouses down by the harbor, and we owned ships that carried olive oil and other cargo to cities like Carthage and Alexandria, and Ostia and Ephesus. We maintained offices and warehouses in those cities where we sold our products. We filled our ships with other products purchased there and brought them back for sale in Leptis.

Most of us lived on our estates up and down the coast, but Jovinus lived in the city. He needed to meet caravan merchants in the forum, and magistrates in the basilica. He needed to be close to the harbor, and close to the imperial officials who regulated the trade in olive oil and wheat. He said the city kept him sharp. He would deliberately annoy my father with references to the leisurely joys of managing a country estate as compared to the pressing urgencies of managing our far flung business operations.

Jovinus was the most worldly of our family. In looking after our interests, he traveled widely. He had seen the Colossus of Rhodes, the Library of Alexandria and the Coliseum of Rome. His experience and knowledge gave him what we Romans call gravitas, a presence at once stern yet somehow wise and understanding; a quality that often caused me to feel as if I was under oath to tell Jovinus the absolute truth when he spoke to me. He asked me thoughtful questions and listened intently to my answers. In return, this made me want to hear whatever he could tell me. He often said little though.

He wore his hair cut short and his face shaved clean. He had what people call a Roman nose, a distinguished beak that set off his eyes and mouth and produced an effect of authority and command.

The harbor was the center of my uncle's world. The harbor was the reason Leptis was built. It is one of the only places along this part of the Libyan coast that offers protection for ships when storms strike, and provides moorings where ships can tie up to load and unload cargo from sturdy warehouses that ring the harbor.

To Leptis came caravans with hundreds of camels from across the desert bringing slaves, ivory, gold, ostrich feathers and exotic animals for export to the rest of the empire. Caravan merchants sold their wares to the trading houses of Leptis who in turn exported this merchandise along with our olive oil and wheat to cities across the sea – Marseilles, Rome, Naples, Aquilla.

Severus enlarged the harbor we already had. He built the new moorings and the sturdy warehouses. And he built a fine tall lighthouse at the harbor entrance. At the top of that lighthouse a bonfire is kept burning day and night during the shipping season from early spring to late fall. Sailors far out at sea can set their course and steer by our beacon.

Oil from the Green Sea

Olive oil is the main reason ships come to our port. And our province of Tripolitania produces oil in amazing abundance. Tripolitania extends from Leptis to the east along the coast road for four days travel, and to the west for four days as well. It extends inland from the coast for a day's travel at least and sometimes two or three. Much of this land has seen the planting and cultivating of olive trees for eight hundred years, maybe more. The result is a forest of olive trees. People call our land the "Ocean of Olive Trees" or the "Green Sea". And Leptis is the harbor on this sea.

There are two other smaller cities on the coast of the green sea. A day's travel west is the city of Oea, and beyond Oea by another day's journey is Sabratha. These two cities with Leptis comprise the three cities that give rise to the name of our province, Tripolitania, land of three cities.

The leaves of the green sea soak up the relentless African sunlight and use its energy to create that most useful of all fruits – the olive. And when the shade of the olive tree shields the land from the full force of the sun, this hard land can be softened. It can be made fertile and productive. Mixed in with the olive trees are fields of wheat and barley, and in the patches of sunlight between the trees, we grow melons and cultivate vegetables.

This green sea of olive trees once produced enough oil every year to pay the annual levy imposed on us by Octavian for supporting Marc Antony in the civil war that brought Octavian to power. Yet even after paying the emperor's levy of 200,000 amphora of oil each year, there was still much more oil to sell to other cities. Raiding and other ravages have reduced the green sea from its peak, yet it remains productive, and olive oil continues to be the life blood of Leptis.

The produce of our estates comes not because of plentiful rain and fertile soil; it comes because of hard work and careful tending of every scarce drop of water that falls from the sky. Over the centuries, the land of the coastal plain and the surrounding hills has been covered with fields and waterworks to collect and channel the rain when it comes. Terraces and retaining walls on the hillsides cause the rain to soak into the earth instead of rushing into the ravines. This waters the olive trees so they grow and shade the land. Water that overflows the terraces is captured in ditches that lead to underground cisterns where it is stored for later use. Water that reaches the ravines is stored behind low dams where it seeps into the ground and waters the crops of the valley floors after the rains have gone. And when the olives are pressed each year the rich stew of skins and pits and olive meat that remains is plowed back into the land to renew its fertility.

The fields, the waterworks, the olive groves, the oil presses, the wheat fields and vineyards, plus the three cities and the harbor of Leptis are the individual parts that work together to create a living creature that is the green sea. This creature is a bountiful producer of food and oil and wine to sustain a good life.

Severus Pays a Visit

In those days when Severus was emperor, while all this monumental building was going on, messengers arrived from Rome encouraging the leading families of Leptis to join in with beautification projects of their own. This soon developed into a contest between wealthy families to finance construction of buildings and monuments and fountains, and to cover everything with fine imported marble.

The families financed a huge triumphal arch at the place where the main thoroughfares of the city intersect; where the main north-south street of the city, the cardo, crosses the east-west coast road, the decumanus. This arch was dedicated to the Severan family and decorated with statues and friezes depicting Severus and his sons Caracalla and Geta riding with him in a chariot as they enter the city. It was completed just in time to greet the emperor on his visit to Leptis in 205, the tenth year of his reign.

All the families wanted to be seen by the emperor in the best light. This was a rare chance to strengthen imperial connections that could thrive for generations. Severus stayed for several weeks in the villa on the coast where he grew up. The citizens of Leptis officially adopted the name Septimianii to show their eager embrace of the emperor's family name and gratitude for the favors he had shown them, and hopefully would continue to show them.

Then a few years after his visit to our city, while many of the building projects were still underway, Severus died unexpectedly while campaigning with the army and his two sons in Britannia. His oldest son Caracalla became emperor and completed the work in Leptis. And when it was finished we had a city to rival any city in the empire. Even the older public buildings and many private houses were newly covered in gleaming marble. The effect was impressive. It was meant to dazzle and overawe. And it did.

People called our city "an emperor's dream on the edge of the desert."

News of Disasters and Battles Lost

Much has changed in the time since Severus was emperor. The Severan Dynasty lasted for the length of the reigns of three more emperors after Severus. There was Caracalla, then Elagabalis and finally Alexander

Severus. Alexander Severus was the last of the Severan line. By that time he and his mother, Julia Mamaea, were not held in high regard by the soldiers. After a string of less than glorious campaigns against barbarians on the Danube frontier, they were both murdered at the legionary base at Carnuntum in Upper Pannonia one fall day in 235.

That set off almost 50 years of what can only be described as military anarchy. After all, it was Severus himself who showed everyone that the army made emperors, not the Senate in Rome any more. Competing generals and their legions fought each other to decide who would become the next emperor. Emperors ascended to the throne, and then in a year or two, or if they were lucky, maybe four or five, they would be assassinated, and the struggle between generals and their legions would commence again.

As generals pulled their legions out of the frontier defenses to march off and fight other generals for the prize of being emperor, they left the boarders undefended. Tribes on the other side of the Rhine and the Danube and our enemies in the east such as the Parthians took notice and launched devastating raids. They plundered and burned and massacred and took what they wanted.

Ships arriving at our harbor carried stories about fleets of Gothic warships raiding the coastal cities of the Black Sea and the Aegean and the eastern Mediterranean. These were cities we knew, cities we traded with, cities such as Athens, Pergamum, and Ephesus. One of the ships that docked in our harbor carried the family of my great, great grandmother Theodora. They came from Ephesus and fled that city as it was plundered by a Gothic fleet.

She told stories of a city left to fend for itself by generals whose legions were fighting and killing other legions instead of our enemies. It seemed incredible. How could this be? How could Roman generals and the legions our taxes went to pay for turn on each other instead? How could the soldiers be so blind to their duty, and so callous to those they were supposed to defend?

Theodora's family owned a large estate on the coast east of Leptis in the plain of the river Cinyps. This is where the only river in Libya that flows all year around empties into the sea. It provides water to irrigate a fertile and sunny plain that is famous for its wheat. Homer himself speaks of the fertile plain of the Cinyps in the Odyssey.

No barbarians raided our city, but fewer and fewer ships docked at our quays. Cities that we traded with were plundered and burned, and it was harder and harder to find markets for our oil and wheat and exotic animals. As the empire was ravaged by soldiers and barbarians, our prosperity declined.

As city fortunes changed it became harder to keep up appearances. The expensive restorations, and all the new buildings, and our obsession with covering everything in marble had been expensive; now that expense came back to haunt us. We fell behind in our annual oil shipments to Rome, and paying our taxes became harder and more complicated. An official was sent out from Rome to oversee our city finances and make sure taxes were collected.

As the years went by, the example of what happened to other cities also made it clear we needed a city wall to defend ourselves in case of attack. A powerful confederation of tribes was forming in the desert, and we did not know if the army would defend us. We could not enclose the whole city, so we abandoned the outlying districts. Those districts had become deserted or thinly populated in any case. People who once lived there lived there no longer. The bustle of activity that once hummed through the harbor and the city, and into the country beyond, had become noticeably less. Where once there were a hundred thousand souls, our city now holds half that number.

We scavenged those districts and monuments that were abandoned for the bricks and building stones to build our wall, and what remains of those areas is more and more covered over by the blowing sand. The farms and olive groves near the city are not tended as they once were; trees have died and raiders have cut them down in acts of vengeance and intimidation. Desert reclaims the land as the sun bakes the naked ground, and the soil goes dry, and the wind blows it away.

Defending the Desert Frontier

In addition to his ambitious plans to embellish our city, Severus also set about securing our city and our lands from raids of the desert tribes to the south. It was decided there should be three big legionary fortresses built far out in the desert to protect the city and our province of Tripolitania. These three fortresses at Bu-Ngem, Cydamie and Ghadamies controlled access to the water sources that raiders would need if they were to cross the desert and raid our cities and farms on the coast.

Building them was a challenge, but not one that could stop Roman engineers and soldiers. A challenge bigger than building the fortresses themselves was feeding and provisioning the hundreds of soldiers who would garrison each fortress. It was one thing to bring up rations to support soldiers on campaign for a month or two. But it was an entirely different matter to support permanent garrisons of soldiers in desolate places far out in the desert.

Severus had an answer to this challenge. He financed the building of dams and cisterns and irrigations works to make the desert valleys bloom. These water management projects made it possible to grow crops that would feed the soldiers. The desert fortresses were part of his program to not only better protect Leptis and the other cities on the Libyan coast, but also to make it possible and profitable to expand the land used for planting and growing olive trees.

More olive trees would produce more oil, and that would feed the ever growing demand for African oil to feed the cities of the empire. This would, of course, increase the wealth and prestige of his family and other wealthy and influential families in his ancestral city.

Although rainfall out in the desert was not sufficient to support farming, when the runoff of that rainfall was carefully collected and concentrated in the desert valley floors, and held by low walls across the valleys so it did not rush to the sea and drain away, then amazing things happened. When the water was allowed to sink into the soil and be stored in underground cisterns for future use, then it was quite possible to grow olive trees and date palms and sow wheat in small irrigated fields.

Severus got the whole process moving by financing the initial desert water works and building the fortresses. In a few years, as the crops began to grow, the soldiers of Legio III Augusta who manned the fortresses provided demand for produce grown in the desert valley farms. A cycle of development was started. The fortresses provided protection for the farmers who provided food for the soldiers. And as soldiers retired they were given plots of land to farm for themselves. The valleys bloomed. Farmers planted date palms, olive trees, wheat, barley, and grapes. They raised goats, cows, horses, and chickens.

Behind this newly strengthened frontier the wealthy families invested their money in further development of the land. They financed the building of similar water management and irrigation works in the hilly semi-desert land between the coast and the frontier. The big estates expanded, slaves were imported, smaller desert tribes were even induced to become settled farmers working on estates or on their own small farms. As the planting of olive trees increased and spread, huge stone piers were erected to anchor olive presses that were built throughout the costal plain and up into the hills that let onto the high desert plateau. A cycle of productivity and prosperity ensued for many decades.

Then the empire turned on itself. During the years of military anarchy constant wars squandered our treasure and destroyed our land and bankrupted our cities. The emperors could no longer afford to maintain the defenses that Severus had established. So the big desert fortresses were abandoned and smaller forts were built further back toward the coast.

The Desert Farmers

In place of regular soldiers in the big fortresses, we turned to the desert farmers, many of them were retired soldiers or their descendents. They were given tax dispensations and weapons and other inducements to take up the job of defending the frontier. For them we created a new class of auxiliary soldiers, they were known as *limitanei* – those who protect the frontier.

They lived in extended family groups and clans in their desert valleys; they were proud of their farms and the lives they had built. Their situation made them more independent and more self-sufficient than the people who lived and farmed closer to the coast. They became the buffer between us and the unpredictable desert tribes.

As the legion fortresses were abandoned, the limitanei left their open farm houses on the valley floors and built new fortified residences on hills and outcrops along the edges of their desert valleys. These new dwellings were sturdy two and three story square stone towers built with small internal courtyards. They were built with fine rounded corners and craftsmanship learned from years of service as legionary soldiers.

These farmers and their sons were still Roman soldiers, but they were not expected to go on campaign, they stayed where they lived and fought only to protect their land. And they were not paid like regular soldiers either; instead they were paid with grants of land and provided with supplies such as armor and weapons and occasional cash dispensations. They also had priority for selling their olive oil and produce to the detachments of regular troops who manned the smaller forts.

Symbols of Regency

At the confluence of two of the bigger valleys in a system of valleys known as the Wadi Zem-Zem there is a town that is the home of a powerful clan of desert farmers who farm those fertile valleys.

It has been over a hundred years since desert farming started. There has been a hundred years of building dams and ditches and sluice gates to collect and channel the desert rainfall into the valley floors. There has been a hundred years of building low walls across the valley floors to slow down and trap the water and give it time to seep deep into the soil. A hundred years of building underground cisterns for storing water to use during the dry seasons; a century of building sturdy stone towers and fortified farms to shelter the farmer families and clans.

The effect of all this is startling, even when one has been told about it and is prepared to be impressed. The green sea we created on the coast has been reproduced by these desert farmers out in the desert; far beyond our ability to regulate or tax them.

My father brought me along with him on a diplomatic mission to visit the limitanei commander of that sector on the frontier. He brought with him several cart loads of weapons and tools as well as a cash donation to the commander in honor of his daughter's wedding that would be held during the time we were there.

And for the groom in this wedding he also brought presents. The groom was the son of a powerful desert chief. That chief was getting old and wished for his son to succeed him. But in order for that to happen, his son had to acquire from Rome the symbols of regency. For centuries these tribes held the empire in awe as a mysterious embodiment of power and authority. Even tribes that were hostile to the empire still considered it necessary for any chief who would rule over them to prove his fitness to rule by acquiring these symbols.

The rule of a chief was legitimized when he received these symbols from a suitable representative of the emperor in a public ceremony. The symbols were a silver baton decorated with gold and sometimes set with jewels, a silver cap held in place with silver bands, a while woolen cape with a golden broach to hold it in place, and an embroidered tunic and gilded leather boots. They were gaudy but effective. They could only be obtained from Rome. There were no other people in their world capable of making such things.

After a three day journey through hot expanses of sandy brown and rocky grey landscapes cut by dry washes and strewn with boulders and clumps of tough thorn bushes, we came on the afternoon of the third day to the edge of a deep, wide and lush green valley. The sudden sight of groves of olive trees and date palms, and the reflection of sunlight from pools of water and irrigation channels was completely unexpected given the surrounding desert.

On the opposite side of the valley along its rim, I took in the sight of the fortified farmsteads with their tall stone towers built close to the valley walls. Looking up the valley to my right I saw the clustering of towers and other buildings became denser at the confluence of two smaller valleys which came together to form this larger valley.

Father was skilled at the endless diplomacy and maneuvering required to keep the desert tribes at bay, and needed to keep the limitanei commanders loyal and committed to our defense. At least committed enough to guard the desert oasis watering wells, and deny that water to would-be tribal raiders.

On arriving at this town, its name is Ghirza, we were greeted by the limitanei commander. He wore his commander's uniform. It was a white linen tunic with red embroidery patterns that extended down his sleeves and loose fitting pants of heavy brown cloth and leather sandals with thick soles. Around his waist was an ornately decorated leather belt with a large brass buckle, and from it hung his sword in a metal scabbard. His skin was tan and swarthy, yet his hair was blond and his eyes were blue.

His great grandfather, my father told me, had been a centurion with the legionary soldiers manning the fort at Bu-Ngem a hundred years ago. He had been a Goth from across the Danube. The Roman army was then and is even now how many Goths win glory and see the world. This man did well and rose in the ranks to command of a unit of 250 men. At the end of his 20 year enlistment period his choice was either to make his way back to a forested river world on the other side of the sea that he had not seen in almost two decades, or accept a grant of land and use his retirement bonus to buy tools and seeds, and build his farm and sell produce back to the army he already knew. He was in his early 40s and still in good health. He decided to stay.

He had already learned the skills of carpentry, stone masonry and blacksmithing from years of doing those things in the army during long periods of peace in between occasional battles and skirmishes. He and his descendants have prospered since. Generations of limitanei have mixed with the sons and daughters of other limitanei, yet even from the beginning, and now increasingly, they mix with the desert tribes. How could it be otherwise?

As Roman soldiers withdrew, the tribes expanded into those spaces that opened up. Over the years the tribes have come to depend on trade with the limitanei for food and olive oil. In return the limitanei acquire exotic goods such as leopard skins, frankincense, ostrich plumes, gold and occasionally even slaves. The tribes also breed fast horses and hardy camels which are always in demand.

On the day following our arrival was the wedding of the daughter of this limitanei commander and the son of a chief of a powerful desert tribe called the Austoriani. This young man was ordained by his father to succeed him as chief, but as custom demanded, he needed to receive the symbols of regency from a Roman official in order to be fully recognized by his tribe as their new chief.

He was accompanied by a large entourage of bodyguards and members of his extended family. In particular, I remember one person in his entourage. My father pointed him out to me. He was a boy about my age, about 11 or 12; he was the younger half brother of this new chief. Protocol held that we should stand together at the ceremony, him and me. The limitanei commander made an introduction between the two of us. I extended my hand, but this young man stared back suddenly and angrily into my eyes and turned away. He did not bother to look at me again. I was to see him some years later under much different circumstances.

The day after the marriage ceremony, the investiture ceremony for the new chief was held. Again crowds of people gathered in the town square. Pledges of friendship and alliance were made by the new chief and translated by the limitanei commander into Latin for my father. In turn my father pledged the friendship of Rome and the recognition of his position as the rightful chief of the Austoriani. The commander translated those words from Latin into the language of the Austoriani.

Then the symbols of regency were brought out with an honor guard of limitanei who emerged from the fortified tower home of the family of their commander. The new chief received them, I thought, with the glee of a child. He was delighted with these offerings. They shone and glittered in the sunlight. And as long as he lived, they announced that he was the chief, and no other contender could take his place, unless we Romans consented to give that contender his own symbols of regency.

That was our hold on these tribes. It was slender, it could be overplayed and broken, but on that trip and others, I learned from my father about the diplomacy and leverage that can be built around such slender holds.

My father was fond of a saying that is attributed to Julius Caesar. Caesar said, "Divide et impera", meaning divide your opponents and rule. We no longer have the strength to attack our enemies openly, but we have clever ways to create rivalries and divisions among them. And with skillful diplomacy, we can induce them to attack each other and keep themselves distracted and disorganized. We have gotten good at this game. We use it with enemies external and internal.

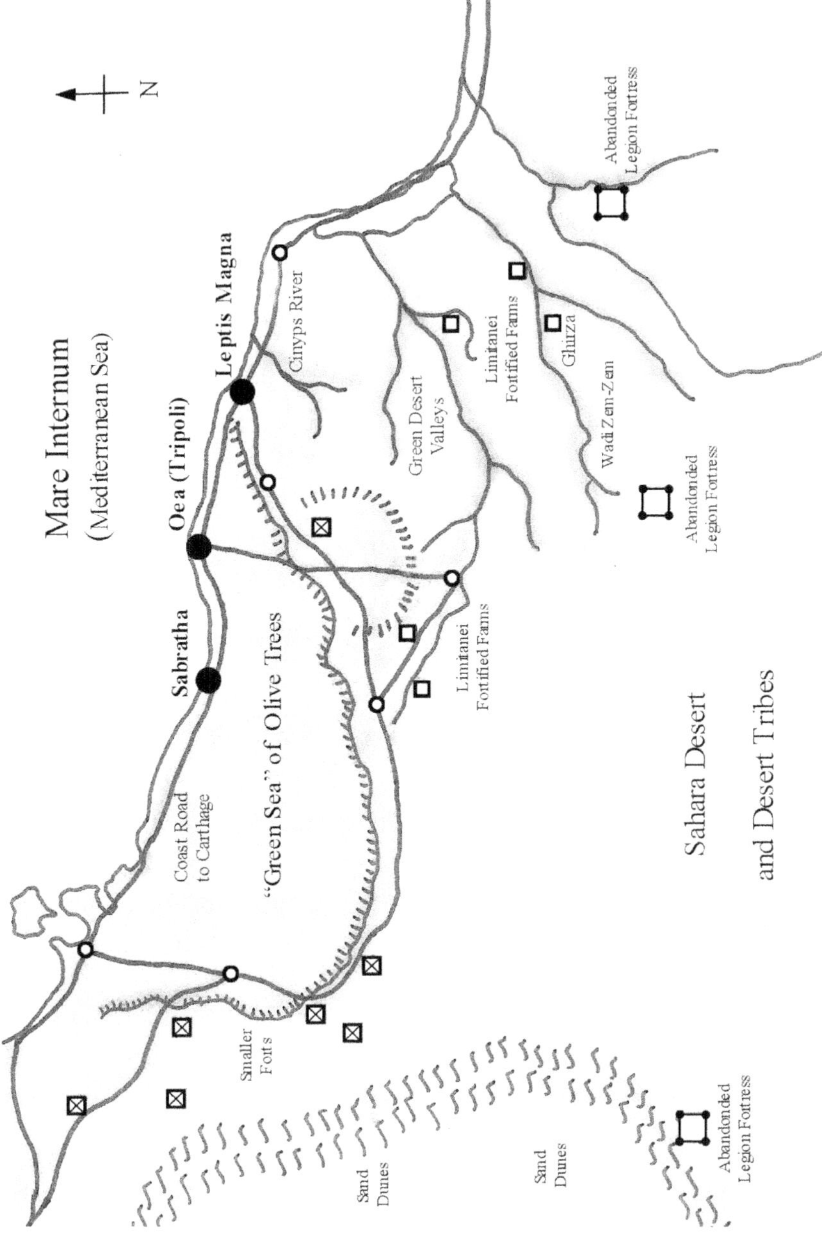

Chapter 3

Game of Extortion

We are a nation of laws but this is made a mockery of by the power of the emperors. The great Octavian Augustus first took the absolute imperial power as a way to save what was then the Roman Republic. We had become ungovernable and felt the need for a single strong man to hold us together. We abdicated our responsibility to find common ground.

People told themselves at the time that Augustus was a good emperor who respected the Senate and the Republican traditions even though he was no longer actually constrained to abide by them. He styled himself "princeps primus" or first among equals. People thought those who followed him in the role of emperor would surly learn from his example and do the same. Alas, the years since have proven us wrong.

The "Carthaginians' revenge" is what they called it when Severus became emperor. The great grandson of a former enemy, son of a Punic aristocratic family, became ruler of Rome. Severus took the Aurelian name and claimed to be the adopted son of Marcus Aurelius and thus part of the Antonine Dynasty. He worked hard to be seen as a continuation of the glory and prosperity that the Antonines represented in the minds of the people. But under Severus, prosperity began to falter.

Dynasty of the Grim African

I was raised on stories of Severus and his two sons and the events that came about after he became emperor. It was the time when the dynasty of Severus made our family royal, and for a time, also divine. The stories understandably are inclined to be kind to Severus and point out his good qualities and good intentions and the reasons why he had to do what he had to do. Consequences of events from that time echo still through the empire.

Behind his back, Severus was called the “Grim African” because of his severe way with people and his short temper. He ruled in the manner of a general commanding a legion, not in the traditional manner of a senator conferring with his respected colleagues. And he made the same fatal mistake made by Marcus Aurelius. Both men persisted in believing their sons could succeed them as emperors. Only a father could be so blind.

Severus had two sons, Caracalla and Geta and neither of them were fit to be emperor but, to make matters worse, he did not choose one over the other, he made them both co-emperors. He always said the theme of his rule was to restore the dignity of the empire, but his actions were to establish a hereditary dynasty based on military power. When he lay on his dying bed at the legionary base at Eboracum in Britannia, it is reported that his last words to his two sons were, “Stick together, pay the soldiers, and to hell with the rest.”

Severus launched a process of disintegration that has ground on inexorably for the last 180 and some years, resulting in the state we find ourselves in today. After Severus died, his sons did not stick together. The elder son, Caracalla, had is younger brother murdered and he became sole emperor. His bother Geta was assassinated at a reconciliation meeting where their mother, Julia Domna, had invited both of them to meet. A story in our family has it that when hidden assassins emerged to attack Geta, he ran to his mother’s arms for protection and was literally killed in her arms. Some even say it was Caracalla himself who killed his brother in his mother's arms.

After this, Caracalla secured his title as sole emperor by doubling the pay of his Praetorian Guard and giving smaller raises and donations of gold to all the soldiers in all the legions. This was no less a buying of the empire than what the wealthy senator Didus Julianus had done when he heaped money on the Praetorian Guard after the murder of Pertinax. Only this time the money used to buy the title of emperor was the money of the state itself instead of the private fortune of a wealthy banker.

The farce that was the Severan dynasty after Severus played itself out over the next 30 years. Caracalla ordered the Senate to pass a decree of damnatio memorai – which is literally to damn the memory of someone, and that someone was his former brother and co-emperor Geta. Geta's name was chiseled out of inscriptions across the empire and his face was erased from pictures and mosaics everywhere.

Caracalla lavished pay on the soldiers and claimed he was one of them. But he was mostly a cruel and vicious young man who killed people on mere suspicion of disloyalty. He made many enemies. At the end of a visit to Alexandria one year, he ordered the massacre of thousands of unarmed Alexandrians for reasons he would never speak about afterwards. Family tradition has it that he was enraged when Alexandrians on several occasions during his visit publically voiced their disapproval of his murder of Geta.

A few years later, while on campaign with the army, Caracalla was assassinated, and the head of his Praetorian Guard briefly became emperor. The story I heard about this is that the army had stopped by the side of the road for a brief rest and Caracalla walked off into the bush to relieve himself. The man in charge of his bodyguard, and also commander of the Praetorian Guard, was a Moor by the name of Macrinus. Macrinus ordered Caracalla's bodyguard to step away to give him privacy while he heeded nature's call. Then, somehow, an archer from a native auxiliary unit whose brother had earlier been executed for disobeying orders, was able to sneak up on Caracalla and shoot several arrows into him. The emperor cried out as this happened of course, and his bodyguard did come running and quickly dispatched the archer, but alas, the damage had been done.

In order to take back the throne from Macrinus, the formidable Severan women from the Syrian side of the family, the Julias we call them, banded together. There was Julia Domna, wife of Severus, her sister Julia Maesa, and her sister's two daughters, Julia Soaemias and Julia Mamaea. They put their skills for intrigue to good use and one after the other, the two daughters had their sons declared emperor. Due to the young ages of both sons, their mothers acted as regents and were the real power behind the thrones of their sons.

Julia Soaemias and her son Elegabalus came from the ancient Syrian city of Emessa. Elegabalus was 14 years old when he was declared emperor. The behavior of the boy and his mother soon shocked and scandalized Roman society. His mother claimed her son was the high priest of Helio-Baal the Sun God, and tried to push this religion on Roman society. Elegabalus himself became known for his flagrant homosexual affaires. It was said he deliberately arranged to be caught in the middle of the sexual act so as to scandalize proper Roman sensibilities. After four years the soldiers killed both of them and cut off their heads and dragged their bodies through the streets of Rome.

Then the mantel fell to Julia Mamaea and her son Alexander Severus. Alexander was only 13, but Julia Mamaea learned something from the fate of her sister. She avoided the sensationalism of her sister and did not let her son act out in public as Elegabalus had. So their reign lasted longer, yet the soldiers continued to be difficult to control and required constant attention and bribes. Finally after 13 years, tensions got out of hand and Julia Mamaea and Alexander Severus were murdered. That was the end of the Severan dynasty. And it was the beginning of decades of constant fighting between army generals and their legions for control of the empire.

Consequences of Anarchy

In claiming to uphold the honor of the empire, my ancestor Severus delivered the final blow to an already wounded ideal that rulers served at the consent of the ruled, not the other way around. In spite of his insistence to the contrary, it was Severus who brought a final end to the golden age, the age of the Antonine dynasty and the Pax Romana, even though he claimed to be an Antonine himself and adopted their name to prove it. What he really proved was that emperors are made by the army, not the Senate. And the army can be bought.

Imagine the spectacle in the years of military anarchy that followed. Roman legions that were paid and equipped to defend the borders and protect the cities, left the borders undefended and marched through the empire on its fine paved roads, requisitioning supplies for which they often did not pay from cities as they passed while on their way to meet and battle other Roman legions from other frontiers to determine whose general would become the next emperor.

More legionaries were killed by other legionaries than by Persians or Goths or Vandals or any other enemies. And while the legions left the borders undefended, those same enemies took full advantage of opportunities to raid and plunder and burn - Athens, Ephesus, Thessalonica, Antioch, all were plundered.

There were many among the noble families and among the soldiers too who saw and understood the tragedy, yet for almost 50 years none were able to stop it. All were caught up in the irresistible logic and urgent compulsion to act as they did in this self-feeding cycle of conflict and destruction. For everyone knew if they did not act first, then others would.

All great empires destroy themselves and ours is no exception. Empires need to fear and guard against their own unrestrained power and greed far more than guarding against the attacks of external enemies. Indeed, when Romans fight Romans and legions battle each other, who are the enemy?

Finally, in 284, a strong Pannonian general was proclaimed emperor by a council of the army's top commanders. His name was Diocletian and he set about restoring the traditional Roman order with the relentless discipline that the life of a soldier can impress upon one. No one dared disobey his edicts, and perhaps the peace of exhaustion had also descended on the empire. Diocletian reunited provinces in the west such as Gaul and Britannia that had fallen under the sway of rogue generals. The Senate in Rome granted him the honorary title of "Restitutor Orbus" – restorer of the world. After 50 years of military chaos, invading tribes and endless civil war, it seemed as if the old order would finally be resurrected.

The Wellborn Few

It took the firm military discipline of Emperor Diocletian to restore the empire. He issued edicts for everything from prices to professional practices. He subdivided the big provinces into many smaller provinces so as to eliminate powerful governors of large provinces who had once, and might again, rise up and attempt to seize the title of emperor. Along with these many smaller provinces also came many small administrators and officials. And the army was expanded as well to defend the borders against ever more aggressive enemies.

Wealthy families had ways and connections to avoid their taxes, so the increased burden of paying for this expansion of the army and the imperial administration fell mostly on the humble people. It was as if families like mine lived in this newly reorganized and peaceful world as honored guests. In the security that once again prevailed, our businesses flourished; the army and the state became steady and profitable customers. We lived on our landed estates; entertained each other and wrote lavish poems and speeches in praise of one another and of the Emperor too for good measure. For a while this arrangement worked quite well, at least for some. Then it began to work less well for everyone except a few.

To keep people on the land and in the villages, it was decreed that if your father was a farmer so too would you be a farmer; if your father was a baker or a cobbler so too would you be. And if your father was a soldier so too would you be a soldier. It became a world run for the benefit of the well-connected, and ruled by soldier emperors who used force and intimidation to hold it together.

Though many of the symbols and names were the same, this was a far cry from the Roman Republic at the peak of its glory in the days of Cicero and Scipio. The republic came to an end when we lost the ability to confer and compromise; when Caesar marched his legions across the Rubicon. But even after that, there was the golden age of the five good emperors, the Antonine Age, the Pax Romana. Diocletian proclaimed a new golden age and a restoration of the eternal empire back to its divinely ordained place in the world.

During the time of military anarchy the emperors had confiscated city revenues throughout the empire to pay for the increased expenses of the army and to keep the state functioning. That practice continued. Because of this, wealthy families no longer wanted to mingle their money with their city's money as it would only be confiscated and spent elsewhere. It would not buy local influence as it once had because it would be spent on people and places hundreds or thousands of miles away. So wealthy families left the cities and withdrew to their country estates. They no longer adorned their cities with new buildings or paid for upkeep of existing buildings and monuments.

We, the wellborn few, passed our days in private worlds on luxurious estates. Is it any wonder the common bond, the identification with each other that held us all together, faded and died? We did not mean for this to happen, but when we withdrew, how could it not? The public spaces of our world, the places that were the home of our common bonds and traditions, they fell into disrepair.

There was no collective we anymore - only contending groups fighting over a dwindling prize, and masses of people simply trying to get by. The concept of citizen was made meaningless when emperors could overrule any law and any due process to attack whoever they deemed an enemy of the state. The whole was no longer greater than the sum of its parts, so the whole began to break down into its parts. And the parts themselves kept breaking down until they found once again some collection of pieces that fit together and created that magic which makes the whole greater than its parts.

The army that was supposed to protect us has become an alien and contemptuous force in our midst. They are one of the contending groups. Noble families no longer serve or command in the army; we leave it to professional soldiers who are mostly Goths and Vandals and Alans and other barbarians who have risen through the ranks. They are schooled in Roman military principles, but they know nothing of Roman cultural life, and have little desire to learn because they already have their own cultures and traditions.

The Christian church grew as the public places crumbled. As the traditional community of city and citizen died, the Christians offered a place for common people to find solace and support. They offered protection against an indifferent and arbitrary world where those without connections and money where left to fend for themselves, and where many did not do well at all.

Our world stretches back a thousand years to Homer and the Iliad and the Odyssey. Our world includes the likes of Alexander the Great and Archimedes and Euclid and Cicero and Scippio and Julius Caesar. And yet as I write these words, I can feel that greatness slipping through the hour glass, quietly, steadily, irreversibly.

Our world is a world of raiding tribes and soldier emperors guarding the borders, of administrators enforcing laws and taxmen ever calling to collect money to pay for this enforced stability that seems to be the only way to keep the world from falling apart completely.

A Relentless Squeeze

Even after the end of the military anarchy and the restoration of Diocletian and the efforts of Constantine who followed him, the economy of the empire continued to decline. Because the cities across the sea held fewer people, demand for our products was also less. The devastation that resulted from the army's incessant fighting with itself had set in motion a cycle of decline that could not be easily reversed. And as demand fell, prices also fell.

Small farmers and minor landowners were relentlessly squeezed. As prices fell, they could no longer grow enough on their limited holdings to earn a living. They fell behind on their taxes and used their land to secure loans they could never pay back. Over the years they were forced to sell their farms to the larger estates and become share-croppers working for the estate owners. A farmer's life is never easy, but when one's spirit is crushed by lose of one's land, and when one's freedom is even further hemmed in by the demands of a new overlord, it can drain the life right out of a person.

The desert farmers watched what happened to the coastal farmers, and became ever more entrenched in their own society of clans and villages and green desert valleys. We needed them to defend us, so we large landowners grudgingly gave them what they wanted when we had to. And we made up for this affront to our dignity by continuing to buy up the smaller olive groves and farms in the coastal plain and hills around our estates.

We concentrated the wealth of the province into ever fewer hands. We diverted a portion of that wealth to pay the desert farmers for protection, and the rest of it we hoarded and spent on our country estates. We built our villas and steam baths and private libraries and banquet halls. We created our own little worlds and entertained each other with lavish parties where we congratulated ourselves for our virtues and our education and our appreciation of fine living.

We withdrew from the cities. We saw no reason to contribute to the upkeep of the public buildings; we let them fall into disrepair. We let the common people fend for themselves. They could negotiate with the Roman tax collectors on their own behalf; we had no desire to risk our carefully hoarded money in the operation or upkeep of cities when we imagined we had everything we needed on our own estates.

And as money concentrated in our hands it stagnated. It was hoarded and not put to use; money was taken out of circulation and locked in our strongboxes. So the common people had less, and spent less, and earned less. And the spreading poverty this caused made those of us who could, hoard even more.

Speaking Truth to Power

In the year 363 the younger half-brother of a chief of the Austoriani tribe traveled freely through our province as was his right since we were in a time of peace. But he used his travels to speak in public places to dispossessed farmers and peasants and poor city tradesmen. He told them they should rise up and make common cause with the desert tribes, and overthrow the oppression of the imperial officials and the wealthy families.

This was clearly rebellion against the state and the emperor. It raised alarms and this troublemaker was arrested and put on trial in the basilica at Leptis. The charges were treason and sedition. These are charges that result in the forfeiture of your life if you are found guilty. I attended his trial in the basilica.

The magistrate who heard the case sat in his dark judge's robes in his seat in the apse at the north end of the basilica. This troublemaker was brought before him. He was dressed in the tribal dress of his kind, dusty wool and linen robes that had shielded him from the sun on many hot days and served to keep him warm on many cold nights. I recognized him; we had met before. This was the one who had snubbed me at the wedding celebration of his older brother.

I heard this man respond to the charges against him. He waxed defiant and even eloquent at times. He had learned enough Latin to speak and get his message across. Witnesses who testified described his actions and established his guilt beyond any doubt. It is likely he knew what the outcome of his trial would be. So he spoke truth to power. He spoke to the assembled commoners in the basilica who came to see his trial as much as he spoke to the magistrate.

I hung back. I did not want to be recognized by him. I remember his words as he described the life of the peasants and trades people of our province. I remember the mockery in his eyes as he described the life that Roman rule imposed. This rule will come to an end he said, it can no longer protect the people it claims as subjects, it can only intimidate and humiliate. A reckoning is at hand he said, "You will learn it is better to be the hawk than the rabbit."

His actions were seditious and his words were treason. The law was clear on his punishment. He was found guilty and sentenced to burn at the stake. Thousands of people watched on the day his sentence was carried out. It was a clear warning to all not to challenge the imperial order.

The Hawk and the Rabbit

For decades the desert tribes had observed the slow weakening of the frontier defenses. They intermarried with the limitanei farmers who were in theory the soldiers entrusted with defending us from those very same tribes. Slowly, slowly, bit by bit, the world in the desert drifted away from our world on the coast, but so gradually did it happen that it did not call attention to itself, and we were not looking.

The execution of this chieftain's brother at Leptis provoked among the tribes a predictable desire for revenge. That revenge was not long in coming. We on the coast were caught completely unaware; there was no warning and no protection from the desert farmers. They simply withdrew into their fortified farms, and let the raiders pass.

It had been several generations since these limitanei had actually served in the regular army, and we gave these auxiliary soldiers less and less in the way of money and equipment as the years went by. They had no reason to risk their lives for us. Whatever common bonds once existed had largely vanished.

Raiding tribesmen swooped suddenly on villas and farms for miles around to the south, east and west of Leptis. For three days they hunted down and killed peasants and farmers in their fields and villages. They looted and burned humble farm houses as well as grand villas and private estates. Landowners caught on their estates were either killed or captured for ransom.

I lived in the city at that time. I was deeply involved in the family business under the careful tutoring of Jovinus. We were meeting with a city magistrate in the basilica that day. There was a great commotion outside in the forum as news of the raid entered the city and spread like gusts of wind down the city streets. The city gates were swung shut and soldiers were turned out to man the towers on the wall. People swarmed up onto the walls and the roofs of tall buildings to get a look at what was happening. I climbed a ladder from the second level gallery up to one of the repair hatches high on the roof of the basilica. I looked along the coast toward the west in the direction of the Villa Selene. It was a fine clear autumn day. All seemed peaceful.

But as I looked to the south and east, columns of smoke begin to rise far in the distance. After a time they started to rise in the west as well.

Streams of people and carts made their way down the coast road toward the city from the east and the west. And coming from the south, columns of refugees and their carts filled the main road leading to the city from the olive groves of the coastal plain and the farms of the foothills. We opened the city gates, and posted soldiers out far enough to give warning if raiders approached. People pushed and shouted to make their way inside the protection of the city walls.

I went to one of the gates and watched as crowds of people passed by. Some were driving herds of cattle and sheep or leading strings of horses. Some were riding in carts clutching a few possessions, many walked. They came carrying the most unlikely and impractical of things, a hair brush and polished mirror, an embroidered woolen shawl, a little puppy carried in a boy's arms, a man hugging two ornate leather books to his chest. These things seemed to have been grabbed at the last minute in a rush to leave; things that had no practical value except that they were a cherished piece of the lives of those who carried them, and they were determined to save something amid the general collapse.

What pieces of my own life could I save? In the noise and commotion of all these frightened people I could forget from moment to moment that my own father and mother, my own brothers and sister in our villa overlooking the sea had very likely been killed or soon would be. Several times I resolved to find a horse and gallop to their aid. And several times I determined to order a squad of soldiers to follow me as I set out on foot.

Yet I knew the blue-eyed Gothic soldiers guarding the walls were not likely to even pay me any attention, let alone obey my orders, important person though I thought I may be. The soldiers lived in a different world. They served their officers and their generals; they worked for pay, and they kept to the company of their own kind. They were there to defend the walls, and not to risk their lives otherwise.

Those who could, fled to the safety of the city. Those who could not, had little chance. People by the thousands lined the tops of the walls encircling the city. I joined them. We watched that day and the two days that followed as farms were torched; trees were cut down; vines were ripped up; and helpless people who did not make it to safety were chased down and killed.

On the morning of the second day there was a great commotion at the western gate. A band of tribesmen had ridden up with a badly wounded prisoner on the back of one of their horses. Just out of arrow range they stopped and pushed the prisoner off his horse. He staggered down the road toward the closed city gate. As he came closer he began to shout. Crowds on the walls moved together toward the gate to hear what he was saying. We recognized him right away. He was a high born and powerful person in Leptis who owned several estates south of the city.

He had been visiting one of his estates, and had given the slip to the raiders at first. But as the day wore on, he grew tired of running and knew he could not reach the city. So as befits a Roman of senatorial birth, he resolved to kill himself instead of allow capture. As a band of raiders approached, he flung himself into a well. In this attempt he broke some ribs and as it turned out, he punctured a lung, but he did not die, and the raiders hauled him out with a rope and brought him to Leptis for ransom.

His wife quickly found her way to a spot on the wall above where he stood and shouted down to him. She was frantic. The raiders proceeded to bargain with her and some others for the ransom they wanted in order to release him. Several times she lowered down to them bundles of gold coins, and jewelry, and silks. Eventually they released him and put the lowered rope around his chest, and people on the wall pulled him up to join his wife. However, we all saw his injuries were severe, and there was nothing to be done for him. He died two days later.

I found others of my extended family, cousins, uncles, aunts and more distant relatives who had made their way into the city or lived already inside the walls. They held out hope that my parents and brothers and sister may have escaped or been taken for ransom. In the days that followed they reminded me that regardless of what happened, we were all family; and the family would live on. “Yes,” I replied.

A man born to senatorial rank has his duty. And he is expected to keep control of his thoughts and emotions even in the most difficult of times. Especially in the most difficult of times.

After the raiders left, I returned to the Villa Selene with a group of our peasants and two of my cousins. It seemed at first that little had changed. Except that it was very quiet. The damage was not so great, a dead donkey and an overturned cart lay on its side next to the gate to our villa. But the villa itself was not burned and did not seem outwardly damaged.

I entered the house, past the mosaic of the four seasons stepping through the hoop of eternity in their endless cycle. A fleeting feeling of comfort and security washed over me. I walked on with one cousin into the main receiving room and was assailed by a sickly sweet smell and the buzzing of insects. A man lay on his stomach in a pool of dried blood; what I did then I do not remember. Did I walk further into the house and find my mother; did I walk past the sleeping rooms and find one of my brothers and my sister; did I walk into the garden and find another brother, and then down the steps onto the beach and find Uta? I do not remember.

I remember following my cousins home. Funerals began in the churches and temples of Leptis. Graveyards were visited every day for weeks. Women wailed, boys and girls cried, men moved about in stunned disbelief that turned to silent, numbing grief.

We sent messengers to Carthage with urgent requests for the Governor of Africa and the commander of the African army to come to our assistance. In this hour of need we most urgently wanted their aid. We appealed to the empire for its protection in our time of distress.

Chapter 4

In Our Time of Need

...AD TRIPOLEOS AFRICANAE PROVINCIAE VENIAMUS AERUMNAS, QUAS (UT ARBITROR) IUSTITIA QUOQUE IPSA DEFLEVIT

...let us come to the sorrows of the African province of Tripolitania, over which (I think) even Justice herself has wept.
Ammianus Marcellinus, Book XXVIII

Down the coast road from the west, from Carthage, came a long column of marching soldiers and wagons. As they came on, from time to time, squadrons of cavalry detached from the main column and cantered over to investigate buildings near the road or groves of trees; finding no reason to be alarmed, they would turn and rejoin the column. Out in front and off to each side of the road, small groups of horsemen kept up with the column by trotting from one vantage point to the next. They kept a constant lookout from hilltops along the route, or bends in the road where they could see far ahead.

The army had arrived. The soldiers were in their marching dress, not their battle armor. They had the distinctive round black caps on their heads that soldiers always wear when they are not wearing their helmets, and their long brown woolen capes were wrapped around their shoulders, some had even pulled up the hoods on their capes to keep their heads warm on this cool autumn day as a wind blew in from the sea. They carried their swords in sheaths at their sides, and they marched with spears over their shoulders. At regular intervals there were groups of wagons drawn by horses and oxen carrying supplies and the soldiers' armor and other equipment. This whole mass moved along at the speed of a man's steady stride.

They turned off the coast road as they approached the city gate and spread out across a large field and the surrounding olive groves a short distance from the city walls. Groups of soldiers and their accompanying wagons arranged themselves in orderly rows, tents went up, and guard posts were established. Hundreds of people crowding the tops of the walls watched this spectacle of discipline and efficiency in awed silence. It was balm for our wounds.

Count Romanus

When the soldiers finished setting up their camp, a deputation of city officials and men from noble families went to greet the commanding general, the Comitis per Africam. This we knew was the newly promoted commanding general for Africa, Count Romanus. Jovinus and other important men led the deputation. I attached myself to this group and watched.

We entered the new army encampment and walked down straight rows of leather tents on our way to a high walled tent with a flat roofed in the center of the camp. That large tent flew the imperial banner of the African army. Count Romanus and a collection of his officers stood in front of the tent and waited to receive us. He was a short, stocky, middle aged man. He was dressed in his general's uniform, a chain mail shirt over a white embroidered linen tunic secured at the waist by an ornately decorated leather belt with a large bronze buckle. Attached to the belt on the left side was a sword and scabbard. He wore red leggings and brown leather boots. On his head he wore the same round cap his soldiers wore, except his cap was made of fine red felt and he had a red cape over his shoulders held by a gold clasp near his neck.

Jovinus and the other leading men of our delegation greeted Romanus and his officers. Introductions were made and pleasantries were exchanged. A city magistrate stepped forward to present Romanus with a written report of the raid and the damage it had inflicted. Romanus handed the report to one of his officers and assured us these matters would have his full attention in the morning.

Over the next several days we got to know more of this new general as he inspected the ruined villas and the burned farms and destroyed olive groves. In meetings with Jovinus and others, I observed his habitual facial expression to be one verging on a smirk that quickly turned into a scowl when he heard something that displeased him. His language was blunt, and at times even menacing. We had come to expect such behavior from the men who commanded our armies.

After his investigation was finished, the city council convened a public meeting in the Severan Basilica to hear the general's report. Romanus arrived to deliver his findings and announce his plans. Flanked by the soldiers of his bodyguard, he strode into the basilica and walked down the central aisle toward the panel of magistrates who sat in their robes on the raised floor of the apse at the north end of the hall. On either side of the main aisle there stood local officials and men and women of important families. The upper galleries on both sides were packed with quiet but attentive crowds of tradesmen and peasants.

Romanus stopped in the space in front of the magistrates and turned to acknowledge the crowd of people behind him. Then his aide stepped forward and began to read a prepared statement from a scroll. As we listened, we heard he would need assistance from Leptis to equip his troops to pursue and punish the desert tribes. Then he went on to request 4,000 camels, and enormous amounts of wheat and olive oil and other supplies. We were speechless.

There was silence in the hall after these demands were read. Our city and lands had just been ravaged and our animals stolen or slaughtered. We could not possibly meet these requests. Several of the city leaders pointed out the destruction we had so recently suffered and wondered where such supplies as these could be found. Others made pleas for help and appeals to his sense of duty.

Romanus was indifferent to our questions and unmoved by our pleas. Perhaps he realized then that he had overreached in his demands, but once he had made them, he would not back down.

He returned to his camp outside the walls and waited for a few more weeks where he received numerous visitors and delegations that came to negotiate and plead. Finally it was clear that the provisions he demanded would not be forthcoming. So, one morning, his soldiers simply struck camp and begin their march back up the coast road to Carthage.

He sat on his horse and listened one last time to our appeals to reason, loyalty, and imperial duty. He responded again with that crooked half smile and those menacing eyes that told us what we needed to know. Then he turned his horse toward the coast road. As he rode off he twisted in his saddle and shouted back, "Call me when you can pay me." And laughed as he turned away.

After these futile negotiations we were left to our own devices. With no threat of punishment, it would be only a matter of time before the desert tribes returned again to take what they had not carried away the first time. We were abandoned to deal with these raiders as best we could.

There was a garrison of soldiers to defend the walls of Leptis, but without the protection of either the limitanei or the regular army to deter the desert tribes, those country estates that had been our family homes for generations were suddenly too dangerous to live on. We needed the city again, and the protection of its walls. Yet how were we to recover the use of our estates? And who would protect the green sea of olive trees that produced the oil which was the reason for our existence and the source of our wealth?

Old Roman Virtues

Could we fight the corruption of the powers that be? Jovinus said yes. In the councils that followed, Jovinus rose time and again to urge that we send a delegation from the city to plead our case directly to the emperor. If the commander of the army in Africa demanded a bribe that we could not pay to do his duty to protect us, then who else could we turn to for protection?

We are Septimiani, the Emperor Severus came from our family and our city. We were staunch supporters of the old ways and the traditional Roman virtues. Jovinus invoked the image of the Five Good Emperors and the golden days of the Antonine Age, those days that are even still the model of how the world should work. We all knew these emperors by heart.

The first of the five good emperors was Nerva who in the year 96 began the process of good rule by setting wise precedents that other emperors followed for the next 84 years. After Nerva, there was Trajan under whose rule the empire reached its greatest size. Then came Hadrian whose reign saw a flowering of Roman culture and the arts. After him came Antoninus Pius who continued in the footsteps of his predecessors; and finally there was Marcus Aurelius, who devoted himself to defending the borders and protecting the empire from invading tribes.

But the Antonine model was based on social virtues and practices of self-restraint that in reality no longer existed. One important practice followed by the Antonines was that they did not promote their own sons to become emperor. Instead, they legally adopted promising young men from senatorial families whom they themselves had appointed to various positions and had seen to be worthy. In this way a succession of qualified men became emperor, yet it was still a hereditary dynasty in a very literal and Roman sense of the word that simple soldiers and citizens could all understand.

Then the emperor who some claim was the best of them all, the embodiment of the Greek and Roman ideal of the virtuous philosopher king, Marcus Aurelius, broke that precedent, and allowed his own weak and incompetent son Commodus to become emperor. His extravagant spendthrift son; this spoiled child forever in the shadow of a father he could never hope to equal, and without the personal strength of character to even try.

Some say it was in the reign of Commodus when the empire began its decline. They say Severus only accelerated, but did not start that decline. Even Commodus, I think, would not recognize what has happened since.

The Soldier Emperor

Jovinus told me he wished me to accompany him if the decision was made to send a delegation to plead our case to the emperor. I was honored that he thought me worthy. In the name of my murdered family and our wounded city I was determined seek justice and do what I could to restore our lives. I imagined high adventure and the honor that would be won. I put on a worldly demeanor.

I had been to Carthage, but never to the cities on the far side of the sea. I was alternately seized with enthusiasm followed by dread. Perhaps we would not need to make this journey after all. Perhaps some wealthy family would find a secret hoard of money they could lend to the city to buy the supplies Romanus had demanded for his help. We all understood the danger inherent in appealing to the emperor over the head of one of his own generals.

Since the restoration of the empire by Diocletian, the soldier emperors had become ever more severe. They are not emperors in the Antonine model, they are not from senatorial families. They do not pretend to be “first among equals.” They are tough soldiers who come from humble origins, and rise through the ranks because of their fierceness as fighters and their ruthlessness as commanders. They expect absolute submission and instant obedience.

The emperors no longer ruled from Rome. They hardly even visited that city any more. They ruled from new imperial capitals at Milan and Constantinople that were closer to the northern frontiers on the Rhine and the Danube. They needed to be close to the soldiers stationed on those frontiers. They needed to see to the defenses, and keep a close watch over the generals who provided the support that kept them in power.

If we were to plead our case to the emperor, we would need to travel soon before the winter storms arrived and ships stopped sailing from Africa to Italy. We would go by ship from Leptis up the coast to Carthage. And in Carthage we would seek passage to Ostia, the harbor of Rome. With luck we could secure passage on one of the large grain ships that carry African wheat and oil to Ostia. Those ships are the biggest ships on the sea, they have two and three masts for sails and with a good wind they can make the voyage across in a matter of only three or four days.

From there we would proceed to Rome and call at the villa our family maintained just outside the city. Then we would travel north up the Via Cassia through the Apennine Mountains until we came upon the wide plains of the Po River. There our road would join the Via Aemilia coming up from Ravenna on the Adriatic Sea. We would follow the Via Aemilia north and west toward the mountains.

Then in several days, with the snow-capped Alps visible in the distance, we would arrive in Milan and the court of the Emperor Valentinian. That was where those who sought influence and favor went to present their petitions. ∞

Court of the Soldier Emperor

Emperor's Dream on the Edge of the Desert

BOOK 2

Chapter 1

Crossing the Mare Internum

On the day of the popular assembly the basilica in Leptis was crowded with anxious people. There was a murmur of response from the crowd as the city magistrates entered and progressed down the center aisle to their seats behind a long table set up on the raised floor of the half-doomed apse at the northern end of the building. People packed the main floor and the side galleries. The second floor galleries were also full to capacity

The magistrates took their places and called the popular assembly to order. The question on everyone's minds was how to respond to the demands made by Count Romanus. Should the city find a way to pay the bribe demanded by Romanus or should an appeal be made directly to the emperor for protection.

Speakers presented ideas supporting both sides of this question. Several speakers reminded us all that Romanus was the man in charge in Africa and the emperor was a long way away. They presented ideas for negotiating with Romanus to pay him certain amounts in return for certain levels of protection. Maybe we did not need him to lead a thousand soldiers on camels out into the desert to do battle with the tribes that raided us. Maybe we just needed soldiers stationed at some advantageous locations in the province so they could respond more quickly if raids happened again.

These speakers made their points well enough; even the simplest tradesman in the upper galleries could appreciate the benefits of reaching an arrangement with the general in charge of the defenses for our province. And yet the unasked second question weighed ever more heavily in peoples' calculations. How much would it cost to pay this protection money? The city and its residents already paid considerable amounts of money to the imperial officials, and much of that money was for the purpose of paying the soldiers and equipping the army that was supposed to defend us. Where would this extra money come from? The commoners were obviously unable to pay more. The money would have to come from the noble families. And each family, of course, had different ideas about how much they should pay.

There was indeed much complication attached to this seemingly pragmatic and simple idea. What other ideas might we consider?

To Play the Cards We are Dealt

Jovinus rose to speak. The hall went quiet. Although he had no official title as a magistrate, he was head of the Septimi, head of the wealthiest and most respected family in Leptis, and as such, everyone was influenced by what he said.

He walked up the main aisle and stopped in front of the magistrates. He addressed them and bowed and then turned to look at all of us. I was standing with others of the family a short distance back on the right side of the aisle. I watched Jovinus turn to address us. He paused before starting. He seemed to make eye contact with all of us in that hall. I was educated in the art of rhetoric; I knew this gesture was for dramatic effect. Yet the effect was to draw us closer to him.

"Fate decides what cards we are dealt," he began, "but we decide how we shall play those cards. The supposed benefits of playing our cards as if our hand was weak are, upon closer inspection, not benefits at all."

"A bargain struck with one who has already refused to honor his existing obligations, is a bargain that will not last long before it too will be broken by demands for even more. In this case honor and common sense both point to the same course of action. One of the cards that every Roman citizen has is the right of appeal to the emperor himself."

"We must play that card. How can our steadfast loyalty to the empire not fail to impress him? How can he not see the truthfulness of our case and look favorably upon our petition?"

With that he stopped. His voice was clear, and it rose in volume as he spoke the last few sentences. When he finished there was silence. His words were short and persuasive. They were difficult words but truthful words. We knew it. Then in the back of the hall or maybe it was from the upper gallery, a child's vice rang out, "Jovinus, savior!"

Everyone broke into cheers and applause. The magistrates smiled and looked at each other. The senior magistrate banged his gavel until the hall quieted down. "By popular acclaim it is decided that Leptis Magna shall send a delegation to plead our case directly with the emperor."

Then the magistrate stopped and looked at Jovinus, "Who would lead this delegation?" Jovinus paused for a moment and bowed his head. Then he looked up at the magistrate, and replied, "It would be my honor to lead this delegation if it is the people's will."

Again, the crowd broke out in cheers and Jovinus turned to the audience and said, "I need a colleague. Who will accompany me and assist me in this undertaking?"

It was understood within the family that if Jovinus was appointed to plead our case to the emperor, I would go with him. It was our place as the leading family. And I found myself anxious to leave Leptis. It was haunted with the ghosts of my parents and siblings. I wanted very much to leave. This was my time to do so. I stepped out of the crowd and made my way down the main aisle toward Jovinus and the magistrates.

I watched the faces of the crowd as they turned to watch me go by. I saw smiles and expressions of relief. Up to that moment I had been utterly wrapped up in myself and my thoughts about death and honor and the right thing to do. I was attempting to live up to the dictates of the old Roman virtues of service and selflessness that my parents and my education had taught me. Suddenly I realized that many others were not so interested in living up to such virtues, and were perfectly willing to have me do it in their name. I saw they were relieved it was me and not they who would make this journey. I took my place with Jovinus and we acknowledged the applause of the crowd.

It was late in the season. We needed to be on our way while there were still ships sailing. After the end of November the storms of winter made the sea too dangerous. Ships stayed in their harbors for the three months of winter.

It was decided we should take with us two golden statues of winged victories to present to the new emperor on his ascension to power. This was the first year of the reign of the new emperor Valentinian. We wanted to take every opportunity to demonstrate our loyalty. We earnestly hoped the emperor would see us as the loyal and obedient subjects that we were, and favor our petition.

There was a delicate diplomacy involved that required considerable skill. This was because the intervention we sought, if it came, might also work against us once we brought this matter to the emperor's attention. There were so few constraints upon the behavior of powerful people, so their actions could easily become capricious and vindictive. We needed to speak fearlessly of the lamentable ruin of our province, and then when this news had stirred him to act, we had to influence the emperor to act in our behalf.

Sea, Wind and Waves

We sailed out beyond the harbor breakwater and into the open sea, the Mare Internum. Life in this place is measured by the rhythm of the waves; the movement of the ship's bow – pointing up to the sky, then down to the water and the waves ahead. It is this rhythmic up and down motion that defines the passage of time. Our ship was a small single-masted merchant ship owned by the family business that transports olive oil to cities on both sides of the sea. The cargo on this trip was hundreds of amphorae filled with olive oil. They were loaded standing up and packed tightly into the ship's hold.

On that morning as we set out, the wind was cold but not so strong as to whip up large waves. We stood about on the deck and stayed out of the way of the crew and the captain as they set about doing the work of sailing us to Carthage. The wind was coming out of the west, from the direction of Carthage. They were the cold winds of approaching winter that are born in the Ocean Sea beyond the Pillars of Hercules.

We worked our way up the coast toward Carthage in long tacks that alternately took us angling far out to sea, and then back in toward land again until I could hear the roar of surf on the rocky coast. I felt a deep unease as the land receded but did my best to keep that feeling to myself. My uncle seemed quite calm so I strove to do the same.

Just as I thought we would entirely lose sight of land, the captain would call out and crewmen on the two big steering oars at the back of the ship pushed forward; the long flat oars swung out and the bow of the ship came around to point once again toward the land. Other sailors scrambled about pulling on ropes and swinging the sail around so as to catch the wind on the new tack. Then the sail was set, and the ropes were secured, the sailors retired back to their places along the railing to wait again for commands to make the next tack. After a time we came in closer and closer to land and the sound of individual waves on the shore could be heard clearly. Once again, just as I began to wonder how close they would dare come, the captain shouted out new orders and the ship again tacked back out to sea. And on we went up the coast.

The wind was steady, and as the day progressed I started to feel more comfortable at least with the rhythm of the voyage, even if I still preferred not to let my mind contemplate where I was and what could happen if the ship were not between me and that deep, dark sea. In the late afternoon as the sun hung lower and lower in the sky ahead of us, the wind picked up and became colder. I found myself wondering, will the captain sail on through the night; how can he navigate without the light of the sun? With relief I heard him give orders to move in closer to the land. He had sailed this coast for many years and knew its contours and its little sheltered bays.

Just as the sun was sending its last redish orange rays of light skimming over the tops of the waves, we came to a small cove protected by a hill that jutted out into the sea. Waves crashed against the windward side of the hill, but on the other side was a sandy crescent of beach protected from the westerly wind. The sailors furled up the big sail and we coasted slowly into this protected nest of calm water for the night. They threw out a heavy stone anchor to hold us there and we came to a halt.

That night we rowed ashore and built a fire on the beach. Dinner was grilled fish that the crew caught during the day with baited hooks on long lines trailed from the back of the ship. We ate the fish with hard crusty bread and olive oil and a pinch of salt, and washed it down with Leptis wine.

After dinner we sat around the fire for a time and Jovinus talked with the captain about the tides and the wind this time of year and our prospects for arriving quickly in Carthage. The captain was optimistic. That was reassuring. We wanted to book passage across the sea on one of the ships of the grain fleet. They would be making their last trips soon before the winter storms began. As I listened to the talk around the fire, the prospect of that voyage across the sea was exciting. And then for a moment, I would hope that for some reason we could just return to Leptis.

Jovinus knew the ways of the world I told myself. I would learn by traveling with him and matching his example. I was an important person in Leptis, yet I sensed it would count for little on the other side of the sea. We rowed back and slept under the stars that night wrapped in our cloaks and blankets on the deck of the ship anchored in the cove.

I lay awake for a time and watched the vast, black sky lit by a shimmering abundance of stars. The rocking of the ship, the sound of the waves beyond the headland, and the smell of the sea brought back powerful memories of the Villa Selene and those who were no longer with me. I awoke several times that night from dreams vividly remembered; dreams of conversations with people I missed terribly. Each time, as I awoke and stared up into the brilliant field of stars above, I saw shooting stars streak silently across the night sky. I told myself these were good omens; they were the spirits of those who loved me and who still looked after me.

One day followed the next and the wind held steady. Late on the afternoon of the fourth day we rounded Cape Bon, a mountainous peninsula sticking out from the African coast, and as we came around, there was Carthage way off in the distance across the bay. The fire of its lighthouse was visible and the wind was such that we were able to set a course straight for that beacon and not tack back and forth. As the sun finally set that evening, we sailed into the harbor of Carthage.

Braving the Deep

The Romans had utterly destroyed Carthage and symbolically plowed salt into its soil after the third Punic War. The Carthaginians had been bitter competitors and enemies of Rome for more than two hundred years and this act was meant to put an end to them once and for all. No one lived in this place for the next hundred years. But the value of its location proved impossible to ignore. It was where trade routes converged and the excellent harbor made it a natural crossing point for ships going between Africa and Italy. It was inevitable that the city would be rebuilt. The new Roman city of Carthage was built on the site of the old Punic city. It came to be as big, or maybe even bigger, than Alexandria. I had been to Carthage several times while growing up.

Carthage was to me the image of a grand and worldly city. It was the capital of Roman Africa.

But there was no time to spend in Carthage now. The day after we arrived, Jovinus went to visit his business connections to see about getting us accommodations on one of the big ships that carried wheat and oil to Rome. Our timing was good.

Two days later a fleet of 24 ships was setting sail for Italy. After calling in some favors and paying a handsome price for passage, accommodations were found for us on one of those ships.

This was the last voyage of the grain fleet for the year. The fleet had to cross the sea, wait at Rome's port of Ostia while its cargo was unloaded, take on other cargo, and then return to Carthage and the safety of its harbor before the storms arrived. Even ships as big as these, were in grave danger if they were caught out at sea by a winter storm.

On the day of our departure we set sail early. The sun was rising but had not yet risen above the mountains of Cape Bon to the east. The sky was pale blue with high clouds reflecting the flaming pink and rose colors of the early morning sun. The sea was still almost black except for pale white foam on the crests of the waves. The fleet left the harbor and headed straight out to sea. There was no tacking back and forth along the coast this time. To our right I could still see the mountains of Cape Bon but behind us the land was receding rapidly. Soon there was no land to be seen in any direction.

Losing sight of land, sight of the place where I had lived my whole life up until that day, and sailing on into an infinity of sky and water had a quality about it that was like faith, faith that there was indeed land on the other side, and faith that I would find my way there even though I had never been there before. It also invoked a good measure of fear related to the consequences of something befalling my ship that might cause it to sink.

On this same ship were several important men whom Jovinus had done business with over the years. Jovinus introduced me to them and the hours passed in long conversations about the prices of wheat and olive oil, about the crops and harvests this year, and observations on dealing with this or that customer or imperial official. Jovinus did not bring up directly the raids that hit Leptis nor did he mention our troubles with Count Romanus. What was there to say to these people that would make any difference? I got the impression that most of them already knew what had happened to us. And the fact that we were traveling to Italy spoke clearly enough about our intentions.

I was grateful for the chance to meet these men and listen to their conversations. It took my mind off what was otherwise an uncomfortable contemplation of sailing across this blue void. Instead, I focused on the tone of voice of each speaker, and watched their facial expressions and watched how Jovinus responded. I was beginning to realize there was much more to business than the growing of crops and the pressing of olives to get the oil. And it all began after that other work was done. By including me in his conversations with these men, Jovinus invited me to learn and become part of those other things.

At night I was grateful for the size of the ship and for our enclosed sleeping cabins in a deck house that covered the back quarter of the ship. We had cabins with bunks built into the cabin walls, and even though it was cold and windy on deck, it was warm enough in our cabins. I slept well in spite of the newness of it all.

About mid-day on the third day land was sighted ahead. Passengers stood in the bow of our ship and other ships in the fleet, and pointed and talked excitedly. The fleet moved in toward the shore then turned and sailed up the coast until we came to the mouth of a river. The port of Rome is where the Tiber empties into the sea. Just past the mouth of the Tiber was the manmade harbor of Rome known as Portus.

The ships lined up in single file as we progressed along the coast, and in that order we sailed slowly, one at a time, into the outer harbor where they then threw out their anchors and reefed up their sails. Across the water we could see the warehouses and loading cranes of the inner harbor. One by one the ships were taken in tow by boats with 12 oars on each side manned by slaves. These boats towed us into a port where we tied up along the quayside of a harbor made in the shape of a giant hexagon, a precise six sided layout that was build hundreds of years earlier by the emperor Trajan to improve the delivery of food to Rome. Gangs of workers began the work of unloading the ships. Cranes powered by slaves in tread wheels lifted sacks of wheat and bundles of amphora out of the holds and swung those loads onto the quay where other workers carried the cargo into nearby warehouses.

We collected our bags and I followed Jovinus down the gang plank. I stepped onto Italian soil. The scene around me made the harbor at Leptis seem small and far away. There were thousands of people; the harbor was ringed with hundreds of one and two story warehouses; there was shouting and jostling everywhere. How could I begin to make sense of this? I stayed close to Jovinus as he made his way through the crowd and the commotion. He knew where he was going.

Along a row of warehouses facing the harbor we walked until we came to a large two story building. Big wooden double doors opened out onto the quay and when I looked inside I could see most of the ground floor was packed with the large amphora we used to export our oil. At the corner of the building where a side street led away from the harbor into the city, I saw our family name on a big wooden sign hanging from the second floor. It proclaimed the quality of our fine oil. The manager of the place came rushing out to greet us when he saw Jovinus. He greeted him profusely and then Jovinus introduced me.

He and Jovinus quickly fell into a discussion about a certain pressing contract to supply oil and issues related to the contract. The details lost me. I stood there and looked about. Seeing this warehouse filled with rows of amphora all with our family seal stamped onto them was comforting. We were important players in the demanding business of feeding the city of Rome. "So this is where the oil from our estates goes," I thought. There was a simple reason for our family wealth.

As I stood watching the commotion around me, a coach was brought up and its driver stopped outside the warehouse and waited for us. Jovinus put his hand on the manager's shoulder and shook his hand and commended him for the fine job he was doing in the service of the family.

We walked out into the fading sunlight and climbed into the coach. Soon we were in a stream of other coaches, and carts and people on foot and horseback making their way along the Via Portuense that runs alongside the Tiber toward Rome.

Coming from Ostia we were on the west side of the river. The center of Rome is on the flat land on the east side of the river and up onto the hills to the east of that. It was dark as we approached the city, and in the sky ahead I could see the reflected glow of the lights of Rome. We stayed west of the river because our family's villa is set on the top of a hill west of the Tiber across from the city center. Our coach turned left off the stone pavement of the Via Portuense and we made our way up a gravel road that wound its way to the top of a hill. I could see a group of people waiting to greet us in front of the house as we approached.

Games, Gladiators and Diversions

The Villa Septimi was a gracious rambling house that spread along the top of a long hill across the river from Rome. Part of the villa and the gardens that surrounded it spilled down the side of the hill facing the river and the city. This was the villa where my ancestor Severus arrived for dinner that night and sat in the imperial chair. The same dining room was still in use.

The Italian branch of the family was headed by Victorianus. He was the same age as my Uncle Jovinus but of a different personality. He did not have that air we call gravitas, yet at the same time he obviously had education and senatorial status, and it was impossible not to like him. Jovinus introduced us and as he greeted me I could see he was working hard to get a smile out of me. He welcomed me to his house and even though that was the first time we had met, he embraced me as his son. That night at dinner I sat in the dining room and wondered about Severus. How bold and confident he must have been to come here to this city and not be overwhelmed by it, indeed be willing to make a public statement about what he intended to do with his career.

That night at dinner Victorianus announced that our arrival was propitious. He said the following day marked the beginning of two days of games to be offered by the honorable senator Anicius Maximus, a member of the powerful Anicii family and an important customer of ours. He looked over at Jovinus and said he would be honored to be seen at the Coliseum tomorrow with both of us. "Maximus will be most interested to visit with you again and to make the acquaintance of Lucius." Jovinus looked at me and back to Victorinus and assured him that we would be honored to accompany him.

I was about to speak up, but I saw Jovinus turn to me and give me a look that was a clear request to remain silent. So I said nothing. Victorianus and his two sons and their friends around the table proceeded to describe the acts and spectacles that would be presented. There would be contests where animals such as bears and bulls were chained together and provoked into fighting each other. Then there would be humans fighting against animals and a particularly interesting contest where a team of three dwarfs would fight against a lion. In between these events would be comedy and clown acts to entertain the crowd while the remains of the last event were dragged out of the arena and the participants in the next event were gotten into position.

At the end of the first day was the most eagerly anticipated event of all. Two well known gladiators would fight to the finish. There was no time limit on the contest and no way out except victory, death or the decision of the crowd. As I listened to this talk I realized these were games that would make the few games I saw over the years in Leptis look like children's play. Although I had seen animals gore each other and professional hunters stalk and kill elephants and leopards in the arena at Leptis, I had not seen gladiators fight each other to the death. Instead those fights would last for a certain length of time, and then if neither gladiator was seriously hurt, a tie would be declared and both would be awarded a small prize. We somehow sensed, although nobody told us explicitly, that the lives of gladiators were expensive and game sponsors were reluctant to pay for that particular spectacle unless they perceived good reasons for doing so.

I have always been earnest in my desire to better myself. Perhaps I was most earnest back then. I applied myself conscientiously to my studies and to learning the family businesses. But it seemed my cousins and their friends had quite a different attitude. The way they talked and boasted at dinner it seemed they had the time to go to the games regularly. They knew many details and had many opinions which they argued over loudly.

I had mixed emotions about the games and what I heard at dinner made me even more apprehensive. But it was also clear from the look that Jovinus gave me that I was going to accompany him tomorrow and there was nothing further to discuss.

The next afternoon Victorianus ordered several coaches, and they pulled up in front of the villa. He and his sons and their friends were in high spirits. Already bets were being made regarding which of the two gladiators would prove victorious. We piled into the coaches and off we went. As we came down the gravel road and turned onto the main road it took us toward the Tiber river and the Pons Aurelius bridge. We crossed over and plunged into the city. We made our way along cobbled streets lined with temples, shops and tenements. The streets were crowded with people. Then the Coliseum loomed up over the building tops, and we emerged into a wide open plaza that surrounded the Coliseum. The noise of the crowd inside echoed off the surrounding buildings and tenement blocks.

The games had been in progress for several hours already. The animal fights and the humans against animals were warm-up acts. Now there was the expectant buzz of the crowd as the clowns finished up their antics by running around each other in circles and crying out in mock fear. We found our seats. They were good seats, they were in a marked box of seats reserved by my family for entertaining friends and guests. We were right above one of the main entrances used by animals and humans who entered the arena. As we sat down a fanfare of trumpets announced the start of the main event.

Two chariots came charging through the entrance below us, a gladiator standing next to the driver in each one. The chariots stopped in the middle of the arena and the gladiators climbed down. They walked back toward us and when they came close the crowd began cheering. The two gladiators then walked in opposite directions around the arena, each raising his arms to the continued cheers of the crowd. When they met again it was in front of the imperial box on the side of the coliseum across from us.

There was no emperor in the imperials box, but the chief imperial official in Rome sat there to represent the emperor and preside over the start of this event. Next to him sat the sponsor of these games. They came together in front of the imperial box, and the two gladiators extended their right arms and cried out the gladiator's salute, *Ave, imperator, morituri te salutant!,* "Hail, emperor, we who are about to die salute you!"

One was dressed as a *retiarius*. He carried a trident, and a dagger in its sheath was attached to his wide leather belt, Over his right shoulder he carried a weighted net that could be thrown at his opponent to ensnare and immobilize him for dispatch with a thrust from his trident or dagger. His head was uncovered; he had only a headband to keep sweat from trickling into his eyes. He wore a plain white tunic and leather straps wrapped around his calves and ankles. His costume was completed with a metal shoulder piece that protected his left shoulder and arm. This type of gladiator with his net was sometimes called the fisherman, the catcher of men's souls.

His opponent was a *secutor*, a gladiator called the chaser because of his role as the one who pursues the retarius. He was armed with a short sword called a gladius and he carried an oval shield. His head was covered by a metal helmet with a visor and he wore a metal greave to protect his left leg. His chest was bare and he wore a short leather skirt held in place with a wide belt and ornate buckle. Around his right arm was wrapped a leather strap.

These two types of gladiators were traditional opponents. Each had their strengths and weaknesses and their distinctive ways of fighting. The secutor was held to be the more respectable of the two because his dress more closely resembled that of a Roman soldier. The retarius was held to be inferior in status because of his bizarre dress and weapons. Yet for this very reason the retarius often inspired the most fanatical devotion and the loudest cheers when he triumphed. As we watched this opening spectacle, one of my cousins made it known to all that he was a proponent of the retarius way of fighting, and announced he had placed a large bet on this gladiator to be the victor.

There was silence in the coliseum. I could tell from the behavior of the crowd that this was indeed going to be a fight to the finish. Everyone watched the two gladiators. A white robed official of the games came out and led the two gladiators to the center of the arena and then he stepped away. The gladiators turned to look as the imperial official rose from his chair and stood at the rail of the imperial box. He raised his right arm and in his hand he held a bright white handkerchief. As his arm came up he paused. Every eye was on the handkerchief held in his hand. Then his fingers opened and the handkerchief fluttered down.

Tens of thousands of heads turned in unison from the imperial official to watch the combat that now ensued. Immediately the secutor lunged forward using his shield to fend off the thrust of his opponent's trident. His short sword stabbed toward the retarius as he advanced. The retarius responded by deftly dancing backwards out of range of the stabbing sword. He kept retreating until he had opened a distance between himself and the slower moving secutor, then while still moving backwards, he twirled his weighted net above his head and cast it toward his oncoming opponent.

The secutor responded by raising his shield to fend off the descending net, but this exposed his unprotected torso, and the retarius immediately attacked this opening with his trident. The crowd roared. My cousin screamed his approval. The secutor twisted sideways to avoid the trident, and the combat between these two continued.

The gladiators circled each other, each fighting in a manner designed to capitalize on the strengths of their type, each seeking to surprise or deceive the other into making a wrong move. Minutes went by. Half an hour went by. The retarius moved the fastest, but as the contest went on, he seemed to tire more than his opponent. Mobility was the ultimate advantage of the retarius and the crowd noticed that he was tiring. Whenever he danced away from the secutor, that more heavily armed gladiator followed after him. The retarius threw his net repeatedly but he failed to ensnare the secutor. After each failed throw, the retarius pulled back his net with a cord that attached it to his belt.

My cousin changed from shouting encouragement at the retarius to shouting criticism and then abuse. "What's the matter with your net you catcher of souls?" he shouted. I gathered that others in our party had also made large bets on the retarius, and they too were becoming angry with his inability to ensnare and stab the secutor.

Both gladiators were tiring. They could not keep up this level of close combat for very much longer. I looked down, and suddenly there was a silence in the ampitheater, a collective intake of breath, followed by a shout from the crowd that brought my head up again. I beheld the sight of the secutor attacking his opponent with one aggressive thrust of his short sword after another, forcing the retarius backward. As he moved backward to avoid that stabbing sword, he stumbled, and his opponent delivered him a swift wounding stroke to his right thigh. I was captivated, I could not look away.

The retarius was now bleeding profusely from the wound he had just received. He fell and struggled backward in the sand of the arena floor. He was unable to get up to continue the contest. The secutor paused. The wounded retarius propped himself up, and raising his right arm with his index finger held straight up, he looked across the arena to the imperial official. In that gesture he appealed for his life.

This official took in the appeal and paused for a moment. There was silence from the crowd. Then the official stood up in the imperial box and spread his arms and looked to the crowd. He turned from his left to his right acknowledging the tens of thousands of people in the audience. The crowd continued in silence for a moment longer as it considered the plea of the wounded gladiator. Then sections of the crowd began rocking back and forth, waving their hands and chanting "death, death, death." The chant was taken up by more and more people until the whole Coliseum rang with that chant.

The wounded gladiator had no helmet to cover his head so I could see his face as he watched the crowd and heard their verdict. He lost his composure. His expression turned to disbelief and then a look of helpless fear. I could not take my eyes off his face. He struggled to regain his composure.

As the chanting continued, he dropped his arm, propped himself up and extended his neck. He bent his head over to the right, exposing the spot at the base of his neck where a single thrust of the sword would sever arteries in the neck and plunge deep into his beating heart. The other gladiator stood over him to deliver this blow that would send a gush of blood spouting out from the wound and bring death quickly thereafter. The chanting of the crowd rose in its fervor.

Via Cassia through the Mountains

There is something about autumn that stirs in me a response that must be similar to the migrating birds, a sadness at the passing of the long warm days of summer combined with a longing to travel great distances, a primal urge triggered by the changing of the sunlight and the shortening of the days. I was relieved we were going to press on and not linger in Rome.

The journey north was an escape. I wanted to distance myself from the scene of my captivation by such naked violence and undisguised fascination with death. I didn't care to review the events of yesterday with my two cousins and their friends. The games would be the main topic of conversation with that crowd for the next month or more. Not only was I was vividly aware of my own response to the combat and the killing, but I was confronted by the nature of the emotions and behaviors the event brought out in me and all the people in the audience. I didn't want to discuss what I saw and what I felt with a group of laughing, mocking young men like my cousins and their friends. I dreaded the repetitive conversations that I would have to endure in silence in order not to offend our hosts or imply disrespect for the business that this branch of the family had been conducting so profitably for so long.

Jovinus hired a coach in Rome to take us on to Milan. It was a large four wheeled coach; each wheel was shod with a hoop of iron that circled the wheel and prevented the hard paving stones of the road from wearing away the wooden wheel. In many places as we traveled those iron hoops had worn grooves in the surface of the road and our wagon wheels often inserted themselves into those well worn grooves producing a somewhat smoother ride for a time.

The coach had a bench in the front for the driver and his assistant. Behind that were four wooden chairs with their legs inserted into slots in the carriage floor, and there was storage for our luggage. Covering the coach was a canvas hood supported by a collapsible wooden frame. We could travel with the hood up, or as we were doing that morning, we could travel with the hood down. The effect of being pulled along by a team of four horses as we left the suburbs of Rome and started our journey north along the Via Cassia was exhilarating, grand, the very expression of how a senator traveled in the empire. This was not how most citizens traveled. Many simply walked. Some rode horses or donkeys. Some rode packed into benches on crowded coaches. In addition to people, there were many two wheeled carts and four wheeled wagons hauling farm produce and other merchandise.

The Via Cassia was one of the great Roman roads built hundreds of years ago. The road was paved with large, flat flagstones, cut so as to fit closely together. It is wide enough for two wagons to pass each other going in opposite directions. It was slightly rounded in its profile. The center was higher and it sloped down on either side so water ran off the paved surface. Underneath the thick paving stones was a layer of fine gravel and underneath that another deeper layer of course gravel. Along either side of the road ran a ditch that carried away the water. This ensured good drainage so the road did not bulge up or sink down over the years as it would have if water were allowed to collect and freeze in the winter and melt in the spring. These roads were built with great effort and care. Rome is the eternal empire, and they were meant to serve her for as long as she needs them.

As the road came to streams, rivers and valleys, there were bridges that carried us over those obstacles without any additional effort. Sometimes the bridges were made entirely of stone. The smaller streams and valleys were spanned by stone arches supporting the stone paved roadway. The bridges were built from massive stone blocks fitted together so carefully they did not need mortar or cement to hold them in place. The larger rivers were crossed by bridges with high stone piers supporting thick wooden beams that carried a roadway of wooden planks topped with sand and gravel. We made our way across the landscape at a steady pace, hour after hour.

By the second day we were traveling up into the Apennine Mountains. I found it enjoyable to climb down from the coach and walk alongside or behind. I could easily keep up with the slow steady pace of the horses on those stretches of road that wound their way up into the long mountain valleys and the passes in between one valley and another. It became colder. The late November air that hovered around the mountain peaks seemed to soak up the sound of our coach and our passing. We traveled into a world where rocky outcrops and mountain tops pushed up from tree covered slopes where the trees were colored in autumn shades of yellow, orange and brown. And clouds moved across the blue sky driven by the same north wind that filled the sails of the ships that brought us across the sea from Carthage.

In between the grey and white clouds sunlight shone brightly and warmed me as I walked. Mountains have the effect of majesty, I feel humble and small in their presence, and in that presence I naturally lower my voice or even tend not speak at all, unless it is to speak of something important. For hours no words were spoken.

Walking beside the coach I could look down the road and up at the mountains. I could watch the patterns of cloud and sky, and listen to the sound of the wind and the calls of the birds. After a time it seemed as if my breath was like the wind, and my vision was the sunlight shining through the parting clouds. Thoughts passing through my mind seemed to be the thoughts of the land itself. Walking in those mountains induced a quiet but alert state of mind that responded to subtle things I would not normally notice. In those times, all seemed well with the world.

The Business of Games

One day as I walked I found myself thinking again of the expression on the face of the doomed retarius. The look in his eyes was a sight that has remained vivid in my mind for all these years. His resolve to fight was suddenly replaced by surprise and desperation as his opponent caught him off guard and then delivered a crippling wound. Yes I was gripped by that sight. I could not look away. And I also felt deep shame at having seen and participated in that spectacle. The sight had gotten into my dreams. I knew I had to come to terms with this experience or it would haunt me. These thoughts swirled through my head as I walked behind the coach.

The next thing I knew Jovinus was walking along side of me. I looked over at him and he smiled, "You seem to be lost in thought. What subject is on your mind that commands such concentration?"

I wondered for a moment about how to reply. I remembered his behavior at the games; how he paid attention and how he commented to those around him at times, but never did he lean forward and shout or wave his arms. What was I to make of this? Did he approve of games or not approve? I had no wish to offend him with my own half formed opinions.

"I am thinking about the moment when one gladiator surprised and wounded the other, and how the wounded gladiator responded to his sudden unkind change of fortune." Jovinus listened and said nothing for a few moments. There was the sound of the coach ahead of us, and I heard the call of a raven come from one of the high rocky outcrops towering over the road. Then he put his hand on my shoulder and said, "You are more sensitive than many. I know you would rather not have come with us to the games. Let me explain some things that you might not have understood."

He continued, "It has been some time since such games were held in the amphitheater at Leptis. That is because there are few reasons to sponsor such entertainment." I replied that I understood. There were few reasons to woe a population to get voted into municipal offices that no longer had money to spend. Jovinus nodded. Unless a city still had money to spend, few wanted to hold any city office because city magistrates were held responsible for the taxes assessed on their city;

they made up the difference out of their own pockets if taxes gathered fell short of the assessed amount.

But, there were still ample reasons for sponsoring such games in a city like Rome, Jovinus explained. As we walked, he painted the larger picture for me. The emotional response that I witnessed in myself and in the crowd was the desired effect, it produced a strong addiction in the viewer. And there was a reason for wanting to addict people to games. Powerful men could sponsor games, and put this addiction to good use to get what they want.

"The annona generates a vast flow of money," said Jovinus. The annona is the name given to the law that states hereditary citizens of Rome are entitled to receive daily allotments of bread and olive oil and other provisions such as wine and vegetables and occasionally even meat when it is available. There were some 400,000 such citizens at that time who could trace their family roots in the city of Rome back to the days of the Emperor Augustus. The magistrate who supervised the money for these provisions was a person of considerable influence. This person, whoever he might be, became perhaps the single largest purchaser of grain in the whole empire. Many people desired to do business with such a person, and many favors were given and reciprocated in the doing of that business. So Roman senatorial families still vied for the favor of the people to win their votes in municipal elections to fill this position. And a most effective way to win public favor was catering to their addiction to games.

Our family did a considerable amount of business supplying the oil and wheat needed for the annona. It was advisable for Uncle Jovinus to be seen at the games presented that day, and it was advisable for me to be seen there with him. The sponsor was one of our largest customers and he had an excellent chance of winning the upcoming city elections. That would make him an even larger customer.

I listened to this explanation. I understood the games were meant to buy favor and influence. There were those who even said the games served to educate the populace in the war-like virtues of armed combat. But I suspected they served mostly as entertainment and not education, and they did so by appealing to interests and emotions that perhaps were not the finest side of the Roman character. Certainly, we all had these emotions and fascinations within us, but are these the things we wanted to bring forth and set loose in a world we wished to call civilized?

What is the satisfaction gotten from this harsh entertainment? What does it say about us? What does it say when fans of the games went so far as to buy tickets to walk among the gladiators at their supper on the night before the games. Fans were not permitted to speak with the gladiators or touch them, but they could watch them eat, or try to eat, what all knew could be their last supper. What attempt was that to connect with strong emotion, high drama, and powerful stories? Did that experience give meaning to their life? Or was it just distraction from their own problems and gloating at the misfortune of others?

Understanding Motives

Each day as we traveled there were villages and inns along the road, and as the afternoons wore on there arose the issue of finding a desirable place to spend the night. Our driver had been over this route many times and knew the accommodations to be had. My uncle and the driver would begin an on again, off again conversation about the merits of continuing to the next village or stopping for the day at a particular inn.

The driver inevitably over stated the amenities to be had at certain inns. But that was part of the game. He had arrangements with certain establishments along the way, as all drivers did, and he sought to deliver as many customers as he could to those places because he would receive a small bonus for each one. The other part of the game that he and Jovinus played was disguised as conversation between a superior and a subordinate. The game was interesting because the obvious behavior of overbearing superior and humble subordinate would not work. In this case the superior was at the mercy of knowledge possessed by the subordinate. This led to more subtle exchanges. And occasionally they culminated in moments when the subordinate would deliver difficult messages and his superior had to judge if he spoke truth or not.

Often the driver engaged in a game of merely telling partial truths to influence Jovinus' decision about where to stay. In these cases, the game for Jovinus was to ask further questions and evaluate answers and try to distinguish real truth from partial truth or exaggeration.

It was not a high stakes game; its outcome would not change the length of our journey by more than a day or two. Yet I sensed an unspoken but good-natured competition between Jovinus and the driver. Each wanted to appear to be the most knowledgeable about how to plan that day's travel and where to spend the night.

It became for all of us a way to pass the afternoons. As I watched exchanges between Jovinus and the driver, I came to see that a good way to decide what was true and what was not, was to judge the level of difficulty for the driver when he delivered his advice.

When the driver agreed with Jovinus' suggestions that was a sign there was no benefit for the driver in doing otherwise and Jovinus had a good enough plan as far as the driver was concerned. When the driver did not agree and delivered messages Jovinus did not want to hear, that was the place for me to pay attention. New information came from difficult messages more than from comfortable agreement. So when the driver delivered a difficult message the issue was to determine if he really believed what he said, or if he was deceiving us to gain a personal benefit.

Two of the days on our journey were memorable for ending with decisions to stay at inns that our driver recommended highly, and which were both notable for their failure to live up to expectations. Both were presented as the harder of several choices, and thus as difficult messages. But we were assured it would be worth the extra effort for us because it would shorten the length of our journey. Did the driver really believe this or was he engaging in a scheme to earn bonuses from these innkeepers at our expense?

Due to the lateness of the hour when we arrived, and the lack of other alternatives, we paid handsome prices on both nights. Our driver made a fine bonus each time I am sure. At one of those inns I looked over from our table at dinner to see the driver and the innkeeper sitting together at a table by the fireplace smiling and toasting each other over mugs of beer.

Understanding peoples' motives for delivering difficult messages was obviously important for making good decisions.

Chapter 2

His Stern Majesty

On the fifth day the road brought us to the top of a rise and suddenly, unexpectedly, spread out below us the sight of a vast open valley. There was the glint of sunlight off water far in the distance where a broad river flowed from the northern mountains down the middle of this valley on its way to the sea. That river was the Po River. It carried the melted snows of the Alps and watered the fertile farmland of this wide valley.

This was where the Via Cassia from Rome met the Via Aemilia coming up from the coast of the Adriatic Sea. The Via Cassia made its way down out of the Apennine Mountains by following the valley of a rocky little river. Several times as we descended, the road crossed on bridges over the rushing waters of this mountain stream running down the center of the valley toward to Po River. As I looked ahead I could see in the distance where the Via Cassia joined with the Via Aemilia. And looking to my left I saw the Via Aemilia stretching off into the distance as it headed north up the valley toward Milan.

I had never seen such broad expanses of fertile, cultivated fields and such abundance of water. The estates we passed along the road went on for mile after mile. The peasants sometimes waved as we passed; often they just stood silently and waited for us to go by. I knew when we had passed from the estate of one family to that of another because the simple embroidery on the tunics of the peasants changed from one color pattern to another. By that measure I determined that one estate required the better part of an entire day for us to travel through it. As we approached Milan the number of different estates decreased, and the size of the estates grew larger.

The Court of Valentinian

On the third day after turning onto the Via Aemelia, we saw the city of Milan in the distance. Our new emperor, Valentinian, had recently divided the empire into two parts, east and west, and turned over the eastern part to his brother Valens who ruled it from Constantinople. Valentinian kept the western part for himself and set up his court at Milan so as to be close to the northern frontiers. It was upon those frontiers along the Rhine and the Danube rivers, and on the soldiers who defended them, that Valentinian needed to keep a close watch.

We had traveled eight days already since leaving Rome. Those were eight additional days that news had to travel from the frontier, and then eight days of further delay for orders traveling back. No emperor had the time to live in Rome any more. The emperors lived close to their soldiers.

Valentinian was a soldier. His father had been a general and he in turn enlisted when he came of age. He rose through the ranks to become a general commanding a division of infantry. After the death of the previous emperor, who was also a general, his fellow officers met in convention near Constantinople and elected Valentinian to be the next emperor. Understandably, in view of suspicions surrounding the sudden death of his predecessor, Valentinian quickly took steps to secure his rule and win the favor of his fellow officers. There was much talk among senatorial families about measures this new emperor had instituted to promote senior army officers into high positions in the imperial government, and also to encourage marriages of high ranking army officers with daughters of noble families.

The day we arrived in Milan was a late fall day of high white clouds and a cold wind out of the north that brought with it more clouds turning heavy and grey as the day progressed. Because of the flatness of the Po Valley plains and the straightness of the road across the plains, it was possible to see the city from many miles away. As we drew closer I could see more and more details. It was endowed with fine and imposing buildings. I could make out the roof lines and features of classical temples and Christian churches, civic basilicas, an amphitheater and many four and five story apartment blocks. Surrounding all this was a high city wall with protruding towers rising above the walls and spaced at regular intervals. A strong fortified gate with a tower on either side showed the point where our road entered the city. Bright imperial pennants waved from flagstaffs on the tops of the towers.

And looming behind the city with its walls and towers was an even more immense presence. Rising in the distance was the front range of the Alps. The tops of the mountains were white with snow. The slopes of the mountains changed color as the snow at their tops gave way to grey rocky ridges which in turn gave way to the autumn browns and oranges of the forested lower slopes.

All around us on the road we traveled there was the vast expanse of farmland. We were like a ship traveling slowly across a brown and tan sea, the colors of farm fields after harvest and frost and just before the onset of the first winter snows.

That vast plain, the increasing grayness of the sky and our steady, measured pace as we approached the city produced again in me the effect of stern majesty. I felt small. I felt the presence of the soldier emperor, the court of Valentinian.

Marshal of the Court

One day shortly after our arrival, we were ushered into the presence of Remegius, marshal of the court of Valentinian. In his role as marshal, he was the keeper of the imperial records and archives. This role put him at the center of many sources of information. He was the chief of the emperor's staff and provided the emperor with reports of events in the provinces. He was the keeper of the imperial appointment book. If one wanted to see the emperor, one had first to explain to Remegius what it was that one wished to see the emperor about.

He wore an expression of perpetual skepticism. He was not a man who wished to be informed that something was not going well, and yet at the same time, he often suspected that indeed, things were not going well.

The reason he did not want to know about such things was simple – if he did not know, then it was not his problem. It remained the problem of someone else. It was his way of delegating responsibility for problems without delegating any of his precious authority to solve those problems. He wished for others to shoulder those burdens. Whether they had the ability to succeed or not was secondary, as long as the matter did not officially become his responsibility.

As I got to know him in that meeting and others during my time at court, I observed a self-righteous smugness about him. He believed his interpretation of events to be the only correct interpretation. He did not feel other points of view were worth considering, and he strove always to find maximum personal benefit in those situations that came to his attention. Thinking of him now, I see it was his naturally suspicious nature combined with his reluctance to accept responsibility that trapped him. Urgent matters often could not be discussed honestly because he did not want to know the details, yet this only served to increase his suspicions and feed his fears. He was embroiled in constant intrigue. He trusted very few, and very few trusted him.

As we entered the meeting chamber Jovinus strode forward to greet him as an equal. They were both from senatorial families. Remegius responded to this as one would respond to a stranger who took inappropriate familiarities with his superior; he simply stepped back, declining to shake hands and clasp arms with Jovinus. Attending on Remegius, standing just behind him, was his secretary. His secretary wore a grin that made me think of an insolent house slave who had wormed his way into his master's confidence. His fingernails were chewed to the quick, and this obvious sign of insecurity made him seem all the more absurd. He stood ready to agree with every remark and opinion expressed by Remegius.

Jovinus presented the documents from the city council that described the raid we had suffered and listed the damages that were inflicted on the city and our estates and olive groves. He related how we had called on the governor and general of Africa. He described the demands made by Count Romanus and the negotiations we had with him to encourage him to protect us from further raids.

As the audience continued, Remegius expressed doubts over the facts of the case and questioned Jovinus closely on several points. How many camels had Romanus requested? Was it really such a large number? Was this not a reasonable request from a general who was being asked to conduct a campaign that would take him deep into the desert to retaliate against the tribes who had committed this raid?

Jovinus replied that some assistance from Leptis was certainly appropriate, but in light of the losses we had suffered, it was absurd to think we could provide the supplies Romanus demanded. That was extortion. Why did we pay our taxes if not to support the army and provide it with the resources to help us in our time of need?

As I watched, I could see the more information Jovinus presented, the more Remegius questioned. Why did Jovinus continue in the face of this rude and overbearing behavior? When Jovinus appealed to a sense of duty to protect the citizens and cities of the empire, Remegius became indifferent. Jovinus seemed not to see this. He continued his presentation as if the truth and reasonableness of his story was self-evident. Why did he not become indignant at the reception we were getting?

Remegius observed that our story sounded like an attempt by Leptis to avoid paying its rightful taxes owed to the general who protected our city. He began using a tone of voice that seemed to go beyond skeptical and became almost mocking. "You claim you could not do anything to help the general in his time of need?" he asked. "You provincials think the paltry taxes you pay should be adequate to do all the things that need to be done to protect you from the enemies that ring our borders." He paused and let this accusation sink in. Then he went on, "You seem to think we are here to come at your beck and call just because you have problems."

Remegius was non-committal about when an opportunity to present this case to the emperor might be had. He suggested perhaps the better course of action would be to return to Africa and take up this petition with the governor or the assistant governor. Our report of raids was not presently supported by any similar report from the governor himself, and the necessary procedure in that case was to seek support from the governor before going to the emperor.

I was at first incredulous that Remegius could so easily dismiss us and our petition. We were after all from a noble family. I was not used to seeing our family's word questioned. Remegius called an end to the meeting by stating that at present the emperor was taken up with pressing matters, and he would see what could be done to schedule an audience. "The emperor will be informed and a full investigation will be undertaken to determine the true facts of the case."

Even I knew that it would be put off in that way people like Remegius have for deceiving and distracting those in power. We left the meeting chamber and walked away in silence. Jovinus waited until we had left the palace grounds before he said a word. As we walked down a quiet side street toward our lodgings in the city, Jovinus nudged me in the ribs and asked, "What do you think?"

I looked at him and the disappointment on my face must have been easy to read. Jovinus laughed, "What did you expect? This is business and in business people act to advance their own interests." He went on, "So the first step in any negotiation is to find out the interests of the other person." Jovinus explained how he had presented different facts to see which ones would be questioned, and how much they would be discounted. He appealed to duty and a sense of civic responsibility to see if this official had any such feelings. Now we knew.

We rented a suitable residence in Milan not far from the palace, and went about the business of making acquaintances and getting to know the personalities and procedures that controlled life at court. As the weeks progressed we were invited to events at the palace where the emperor was present, though it was not possible on those occasions to approach or speak to him.

Favor of a Princess

I soon understood why people wanted to be at court. It was where one had the feeling of endless possibilities if one could just get connected into the right networks. And so there was the unceasing activity of people working on connecting with the right networks. For me the spectacle was such that all I did for some weeks was follow Jovinus and keep my eyes open. As the days went by, I began to feel I at least knew my way around the public spaces of the palace and the city, and I began to recognize people who for some reason or other, I felt a connection with.

I began to participate in less exclusive yet friendly networks at court were I met other sons of senatorial families, and got word of events and ceremonies that were open for us to attend. It soon became my habit to attend whenever I could. It was the way to see high officials and Valentinian himself and participate in some way in court life. But seeing high officials and emperors soon became only one interest when I went to court.

The first time I saw her, she was at some official ceremony in a crowd of court officials and their families. People were clustered about the throne standing in attendance on the Emperor. She looked over at me as

I crossed the room with Jovinus. I looked back. She looked me in the eye for a moment and turned away.

I don't know what more worldly men call that kind of glance. It says in a flash, "I see you. You interest me," and it ends with the command, "Notice me!" Such a glance goes in through my eyes and lodges itself somewhere in the back of my head and starts taking on a life of its own.

From that day forward, as I was out and about, I always kept an eye open for her. I scanned crowds and rooms. When I saw her I found some reason to move toward her and sometimes I thought of a reason to speak to her. When I did, she would fix her mysterious eyes on me and her face took on an expression that made me feel as if her whole being was focused on me while I talked. I talked just to feel her attention on me. And when I made her smile or laugh, it was like clouds parting and sunlight shinning through.

Regina was her name, a Pannonian-Italian beauty. She had shinny black hair that fell in curls to her shoulders. The curve of her hips and swell of her breast were handsome, yet it was her eyes that caught me, indeed they hypnotized me. Her dark eyes seemed to sweep up and back toward her ears, subtly accented with skillful use of makeup to accentuate the mystery of what those eyes could see. It seemed her eyes could see past whatever brave expression I tried to wear on my face, and were able to ascertain my true emotions. It was only later that I realized how obvious my emotions must have been. I wore my heart on my sleeve as the saying goes. When she fixed her gaze on me I found it hard to remember to breathe.

As the weeks went by, and she saw my hopelessly eager attempts to please her, she revealed a lighter and more playfully spontaneous side. I was taken completely. She laughed more often, and I reveled in her attention. Stand with me, listen to me, engage with me and show me the favor of your smile. Brush close to me, touch my arm with your hand, and let me smell the fragrance of your long dark hair.

As I learned quickly enough, she was the daughter of a noble Italian mother and her father was Remegius. It was known at court that he had plans for her. She was to marry a nephew of Emperor Valentinian. She would be another link in the web of connections that successful court officials wove to connect themselves with the sources of power and money.

We were two souls who were not destined to be together for long but the mutual attraction was undeniable. We took precautions to stay out of sight when we were together. Yet thinking of it now, there clearly must be an angel who watches out over young men and women and keeps them safe. If her father had been aware that I was showing her this attention, and that she was reciprocating my attention, there would have been hell to pay or worse, I am sure.

In the months before Jovinus finally got his audience with the emperor I took every opportunity to find Regina and speak with her and admire her and bask in her presence. I am a thoughtful man and was so even then. I knew this attraction I felt went beyond any rational attempt to explain. I let myself be swept away by it.

Regina knew this was only a dalliance. She was already spoken for until her father said otherwise, and in any case, she had no intention of moving to Africa. So when we were together time was condensed into intense conversations, meaningful gazes and touches. Sometimes there was a kiss. And then it would be time to part. She would suddenly remember an important errand or meeting, or any reason at all to run off as quickly as she had appeared. It left me flopping about like a fish out of water; emotions surging through my body.

I came to feel foolish about my behavior and my insistent desire to see her. "Lucius get a hold on yourself," I would say in exasperation. I would resolve not to see her, and force myself to stop looking for her everywhere I went. But in those times when I turned away from her, it seemed as if she would turn to me. How else could I explain her sudden appearance places I least expected her; or in a place where I had just looked and not seen her a moment ago?

When this happened, my resolve to maintain my composure would last for a minute or two; and then all it took was a meaningful look from her or a laugh, and my heart would break open with a pleading intensity, and once again I simply adored her. Until, of course, she would remember some pressing appointment and rush off leaving me again, the flopping fish gasping for breath.

In spite of my sternest statements to myself about the absurdity of the situation and the need to keep this young lady at arms length, I found myself utterly unable to resist her. Yet because of this dalliance, I did hear much choice and valuable gossip that could be traded with other people for large measures of personal prestige and return favors.

Further Refinement of Noble Families

One topic I heard much about from Regina was the countless stories of social maneuvering that occurred as the rich and noble families of the empire encountered the strong and powerful new generals and imperial officials. There was an ever shifting dance as both parties sought to assess and merge with the other for carefully calculated mutual benefits.

Along with the subdividing of the old provinces into smaller ones so as to exert more control, Emperor Valentinian now introduced a more finely graded subdividing of the social hierarchy. Where once there were senators, equestrians, plebeians, freedmen and slaves, now, especially at the upper end of society, there was a more refined and controlling hierarchy. As the old titles were acquired by more and more people they lost some of their exclusivity, so new titles were introduced.

The elite of the human race were those of senatorial families like mine. Yet this included all the families of senatorial rank throughout the empire, and all of their offspring and descendants through the ages. Since the reign of Constantine these families had been known collectively as *clarissimi.* Now Valentinian introduced further definitions of rank. Rising in a pyramid with *clarissimi* at the base, the next level was *spectabiles*, and at the top of the pyramid was the exalted level of the *illustres*. It was also possible to add the superlative *vir* to any of these levels so as to create a higher degree of person even within the same level.

Because of our ancestor Severus, our family achieved the rank of *vir clarissimi,* but that, I learned, earned little respect in a court populated by families of *spectabiles* and *illustres*. The great game pursued by these families was the plotting and arranging of marriages. The object was to combine and increase the fortunes of families and their holdings so as to strengthen and protect the status and influence of these families. Remegius had a beautiful daughter and a marriage of this daughter to the emperor's nephew would be a defining achievement in his life. His family would advance to new levels of social prominence, and he would become a member of that group that is the select of the select.

Since in many ways the army and the imperial administrators now ran the affairs of the world, this sub-dividing of the senatorial ranks proved very effective in channeling the money, energy and ambitions of wealthy families into endless schemes to climb this pyramid or prevent others from doing the same. It became a game one could not resist. It meant the constant currying of favor with generals and administrators and the emperors themselves. Bribes flowed freely. Each got what they wanted.

A New Model Administrator

Remegius shared the background and behaviors of many newly promoted men who surrounded the emperor and held important positions in the imperial government. I learned that Romanus was a kinsman related by marriage to the family of Remegius. They were both of Pannonian heritage, and both had used their positions to marry into noble families. They used their influence to reinvigorate their new family's fortunes and increase its wealth. In return, they and their heirs wrapped themselves in the history and prestige of the noble family names thus acquired. They took to themselves that history and prestige as if it had been theirs for endless generations.

Remegius was calculating and watchful. He had little of the traditional senatorial education, that reading of the classics and training in rhetoric and law. But he was no fool and he had a good head for numbers. He learned to exert considerable influence over the moods and decisions of the emperor.

He protected himself from his lack of traditional education by becoming a devout Christian. He had the sign of the cross embroidered into the designs on his official robes of office as did many other high court officials who were also Christians. Although the emperor carefully maintained his neutrality on matters of religion, Christianity had been the semi-official religion of the empire since the days of the emperor Constantine. All emperors since Constantine, except one, had openly proclaimed their belief in and support of the Christian religion. Remegius did not trouble himself with questions of morality and sin. He adopted his faith as a shield and a sword to protect him against the uncertainty of a changing world, and to use as justification for his narrow pursuit of personal advancement.

He had no sense of obligation to those less well off. This was a man who found additional money to buy food and wine for the emperor's Christmas banquets that year by simply not paying the modest imperial donatives that were normally granted at that time of year to the tradesmen and servants who did the daily work of the palace and grounds. "Perhaps giving them less will make them more grateful for what they do have," he announced.

Remegius spent most of his waking hours moving his money around from one scheme to another, and cultivating the favor of those whose help he would need to continue his quest for more money and more power.

Picture of the Emperor

Valentinian had a strong muscular build from his life in the army and his time spent on campaigns and leading troops in battle. He had a full head of gleaming black hair and grey eyes that fixed upon a man and held him as if he where physically restrained. As he rose through the ranks, he developed a fearsome gaze that he could sweep from one person to another. Its effect was to quickly induce silence and submission.

The day after he was elected emperor by the council of generals he was presented to the assembled troops. From their murmurings and restive behavior he saw the soldiers were not entirely in a mood to accept his appointment. He mounted the steps of the rostrum set up for this occasion and took control of the situation before it got further out of hand. His voice was strong and his words were clear, "Gallent defenders of our provinces, it is and always will be my pride and boast that I owe to your courage the rule of the Roman world; a post that I neither desired nor sought, but for which you have judged me to be the best qualified."

The angry muttering of the soldiers quieted down as they turned their attention to the words he was speaking. He continued on with a short and vigorous speech that combined more praise for the soldiers with simple statements of his intent to strengthen the defenses of the empire and rebuild the army. He ended his address with the promise, "You shall receive without further delay what is due to you for my nomination as Emperor!"

There was silence. Valentinian stood motionless on the rostrum looking out over the assembled troops. His hands were on his hips in a show of authority and his only motion was the slow turning of his head as he scanned the faces of the soldiers. Suddenly a cheer broke out from a section on his right. Other units took up the cheer. Within minutes the soldiers in their thousands where cheering and shouting their support for the new emperor.

As emperor, Valentinian attempted at first to display the mildness and merciful behavior that the philosophers recommend as the best deportment for a wise and powerful ruler. Yet his naturally hot temper often broke through this façade. And once broken through, it goaded him on to displays of frightening rage. He was rarely content with slight or symbolic punishments sometimes used by emperors in times past. Instead he was prone to severity and often ordered wide investigations that ensnared innocent and guilty alike. Many cruel tortures were used to extract confessions from these people ensuring that their trials would find them guilty, and executions would follow.

His temper grew on him as he gave vent to it. In giving vent to such emotions, they came to rule his behavior. His anger became an incurable cancer eating away at his ability to think clearly or logically. It became his habit to respond to any bit of news that he did not approve of with anger. And that could quickly become full blown rage if the bearer of the news was not able to respond so as to defuse the tension it created.

Life in the army had bred certain behaviors that defined his character. He expected instant and total obedience to his orders, and when he became emperor he extended this expectation from his soldiers to all the subjects of his empire. As he consolidated his power he came to suspect that those who disagreed with him did so out of sinister motives, so he actively removed from his presence those people who had opinions different from his own. He had no use for those who were better educated than he, or who dressed in finer clothes or who came from noble families. In the presence of senators and noble families he made no pretense of being, "first among equals," as our first emperor,

Octavian Augustus, had advised so many years ago when the Republic came to an end and the Empire was established.

Gold Dust and Innocence

Some weeks after the start of the New Year, when snow still lay heavily on the ground, a banquet was held in honor of the visit by a powerful king of one of the Gothic tribes across the Rhine. He had come to renew his treaty of peace and friendship with the empire. We went to the palace that evening and entered the hall where the banquet was taking place. Long banquet tables were set and food and drink was already out upon the tables. We were shown to our seats at a table toward the back of the hall.

We had not been seated long before brass trumpets announced the entry of the emperor and the Gothic king. Valentinian was dressed in the uniform of a general. His tunic was elaborately embroidered with the imperial colors of purple and gold. But it was the Gothic king who caught our attention. He was dressed in the barbarian style; a leather tunic with gold thread embroidery trimmed with fur and a woolen cape also trimmed in fur and held in place over his shoulders with a large golden clasp on his left shoulder. He seemed quite pleased with himself as he walked beside Valentinian and saw the attention he drew from the assembled crowd. The two of them took their places in large cushioned chairs set up at the middle of the head table in front of the hall.

Clearly the Gothic king felt he had upstaged his host and was enjoying the experience. Servants scurried about pouring wine into their cups and serving up plates of steaming meat and warm fresh bread and assorted delicacies created for the occasion. Then just as those at the head table began their meal and the rest of us followed in turn at our tables, there was a commotion from behind the head table. Behind the head table was a large double door leading to a hallway and the palace kitchens beyond that. We heard a rumbling noise as if wagons were being drawn through the hallway.

Emerging from the doorway there came two big cages with iron bars and wooden floors and tops. The cages were mounted on wagon wheels and in each one was a large black bear pacing pack and forth and snarling as they pushed their snouts through the bars of their cages. A cage was wheeled to either end of the table and parked slightly behind Valentinian's chair. The expression on the Gothic king's face went from surprise to fear. After a few moments it was replaced with a look of deference and a nervous turning of his head as the king glanced around to see if any other surprises were about to be sprung on him. During the course of the dinner Valentinian turned occasionally to toss choice chunks of meat to his bears.

Jovinus turned to one of our table companions and remarked what noble beasts they were and how they enhanced the imperial majesty. We were informed that they were the emperor's pets; one was named Gold Dust and the other was Innocence. The emperor was devoted to these bears. He often placed them in their cages near his table at dinners of state, and at night he had them just outside the door of his bedroom. We also heard how in moments of imperial rage more than one unfortunate person had been introduced into their presence.

A few weeks later there was an incident when a palace guard had been found asleep at his post. He was immediately locked up in the palace prison. Word of this spread rapidly through court; there was much speculation as to what might happen next. At the time it puzzled me why so much interest and gossip was generated by such a trivial event. I soon found out. People followed what happened next with the same intense fascination I had seen at the games in Rome.

After several days of mounting anticipation the emperor was informed of this soldier and his misconduct. The commander of the guards was called into his presence immediately. In a private session that was quickly reported throughout the palace from several knowledgeable sources, we heard how this meeting had turned into a dangerous tirade. The emperor made it clear to the commander what he expected of his guards. The veins in the emperor's neck stood out, his voice rose in intensity, and his expressions became ever more fierce. "Let Innocence make an example of this slovenly soldier!" he shouted.

That afternoon the bewildered soldier was led unarmed to the entrance of a small courtyard in the interior of the palace where the entrances had been blocked. He was pushed into the courtyard and the soldiers who brought him there quickly retreated and shut the door behind them. It was said later, by those who witnessed this scene from various safe locations, that for a moment the soldier seemed to believe he had been released. He started to walk across the courtyard toward a door on the other side. Then a sudden movement caught his eye and he turned to see the emperor's bear Innocence lunge toward him from a corner where she had been hidden in the shadows. His screams were heard throughout that part of the palace.

Valentinian punished the slightest offenses of the common soldiers, but often turned a blind eye to the far more serious offenses committed by his generals. This made him feared by the rank and file, and it won him support from high ranking officers. It also fed the arrogance and greed of those officers.

Chapter 3

The Inquest

The snows began to melt and the days got longer. The month of March brought with it the first stirrings of activity in the farm fields around Milan, and it also brought news from across the sea. The first brave ships were venturing out again from their winter harbors, and with them came reports from the governor of Africa. There had been more raids on our province, more destruction and death, and this time the killing of three imperial officials who were caught unexpectedly while traveling beyond the protection of city walls.

This was not welcome news, yet it provided the evidence we needed to strengthen our case. And the source of this news was the governor of Africa himself, an imperial official who could not be so easily ignored. This forced the hand of Remegius. A date was soon announced for us to present our petition to Valentinian.

Audience with Valentinian

On the appointed day, we walked down the length of the imperial basilica and stopped ten paces in front of the emperor. As we had been instructed, we dropped to one knee and bowed our heads. Upon a word from Remegius we stood up again. "We come to deliver to you two gold statues from Leptis Magna as tokens of our loyalty and our expressions of joy at your accession to the imperial honor," said Jovinus.

The emperor sat on a raised platform in an elaborately carved dark wooden chair inlaid with gold and ivory. Valentinian looked at us and said not a word. He made eye contact with us and nodded his head. At this sign Jovinus stepped forward again and I followed. We each carried one of the winged victories that the families of Leptis had contributed to and which had been hurriedly cast and polished before we left on our journey. We placed them on a polished wooden table in front and to the side of the emperor's platform. And then we stepped back again.

Jovinus took a rolled paprus document from a leather carrying case slung over his shoulder. He began his presentation, "We your loyal subjects of Leptis Magna present a petition signed by the city magistrates to attest to its veracity. Our city suffered grievous harm at the hands of raiding desert tribes and we seek your imperial protection." He paused and looked at Valentinian who watched but said nothing. Again Valentinian nodded his head. Jovinus continued, "We bring our case to you because the Count of Africa has rebuffed us in our appeals for protection from these raiders."

"Our estates have been burned, our olive trees cut down, our vines ripped up and our animals stolen or killed. Now because of the lack of punishment, these desert tribes have no fear and have come again into our province and destroyed even more and taken that which they did not steal the first time. They have killed commoners, magistrates and imperial officials. We stand ready to provide supplies to our brave soldiers in their pursuit of these raiders, but in our hour of need we cannot produce the unreasonably large quantities of animals, wagons and provisions that were demanded by Count Romanus before he would act on our behalf."

For the first time the emperor spoke. "And what is this unreasonably large quantity of animals and provisions that was requested of you?"

"We were requested to provide 4,000 camels and hundreds of wagons loaded with wheat and oil. Romanus would not consider the offers of smaller quantities that we were able to provide…"

"No my Lord", interjected Remegius. "They exaggerate their story. My sources and reports indicate Romanus asked for a mere 400 camels, not 4,000. They paint themselves as victims and attempt to avoid their duty to provide the army with reasonable support to carry out a campaign in their behalf. It was their foolish behavior that created this problem in the first place."

The sudden intervention of Remegius caught me quite by surprise. Remegius was standing quietly on the emperor's right side next to the imperial chair. This audience with the emperor was supposed to be our time to tell our story and plead our case without interruption. It was not supposed to be like a proceeding in open court where a claimant's plea would be refuted and the claimant had to vigorously defend his case.

I looked over at Jovinus. He remained impassive. I tried to compose my face as well and attempted to hide my surprise. Remegius continued, "You know how citizens expect soldiers to be at their beck and call when they need protection, but otherwise they don't want to contribute to the expenses of defending our borders and paying the troops. My sources from Africa tell me there were no raids beyond the usual small incidents here and there. These charges are simply slander spread by old senatorial families because they resent the rise of new men such as Romanus and even yourself Majesty."

Jovinus now responded, "Why, Your Majesty, would I take time from my pressing affairs to make this lengthy journey and pursue a course of action that has no benefit to me at all unless the raids I describe did indeed actually happen? And if I did have a vendetta against Count Romanus, which I do not, for what reason other than the one I have presented, could I possibly have been provoked into such a vendetta? My family and our city have always been loyal supporters of the empire."

"Your Excellency, I believe this is an attempt to involve the imperial office in the settlement of a personal feud and as such, it is beneath your dignity to concern yourself. It should be referred back to the proper authorities in Carthage to deal with." At this suggestion Valentinian paused. Remegius continued on in the way he had learned so well to distract the emperor's attention from one thing and send it off in a different direction. "Furthermore," he said, "you must not be taken in by this fabrication when there are reports of unrest and raiding by the Gothic tribes on the Rhine."

This last sentence produced the desired effect. Valentinian turned to Remegius and questioned him for details of this new outbreak of Gothic unrest. As he heard more about these disturbances he became visibly concerned and asked Remegius for thoughts on how his troops might best be deployed to counter those incursions. During that time it was as if we did not exist. The emperor was totally absorbed in contemplation of this new problem.

Jovinus waited quietly. Then during a pause in the exchange between Remegius and the emperor, he shifted his weight ever so slightly and cleared his throat. He shifted the paprus scroll with our petition from on hand to the other. Valentinian again turned his attention back to us.

Jovinus looked from the emperor to Remegius and said nothing. The emperor also turned to look at Remegius. Remegius shrugged his shoulders and replied, "As I have said, there is some question as to the accuracy of the facts they present. I believe this matter should be referred back to the authorities in Carthage."

Valentinian was silent. He looked at us. I could see the suspicion in his eyes. "It is our wish that these allegations be further investigated. These are serious matters and we will appoint a special envoy of the court to accompany you back to Africa. He will see for himself if the situation you describe is accurate or exaggerated." He turned to Remegius and gave his instructions. "Palladius will be my envoy. He will journey to Leptis and make a full investigation of these claims."

At that Jovinus stepped back two steps and bowed. I did the same. Our audience was over. This was not the outcome I had hoped for. There was no longer much pretence of imperial concern for the protection of distressed citizens and their cities. This was about the desire of a powerful man to defend his holdings so as to insure the steady flow of taxes and supplies needed for his army. We were there to support the army, not the other way around. That army had to protect us in order for us to serve its interests, and that was the primary reason the emperor cared about our case.

When Truth Cannot be Seen

The audience with the emperor made clear for me the problems and dangers of speaking truth to power. It is the difficult messages that a subordinate must sometimes deliver to a superior that cause these problems. No superior wishes to hear that something he is responsible for is not going well. Superiors are inclined to deny news that all is not well, even if they secretly suspect something is amiss.

So the question becomes how can a superior overcome their natural reluctance to hear bad news and still reliably discern the motives of those who bring them such news? For in addition to hearing bad news, one needs to evaluate the motives of the teller of this news in order to arrive at some approximation of the truth.

From my days at court overhearing conversations when no one knew I was listening, I learned many things I had not known before. It seems so obvious to me now, yet I was innocent of such knowledge then. One afternoon while wandering about making myself inconspicuous and hoping to see Regina, I overheard the conversation of two army officers. They were discussing the merits of demanding additional supplies from city magistrates to supplement the cash allowances and provisions that were already sent to them.

In hearing this conversation I realized Romanus was extorting supplies from the African cities he was supposed to protect, and pocketing the money sent to him by the imperial government to purchase those supplies. I realized this extortion and diversion of money must be a common fraud engaged in by many who were in positions to do so. For Romanus this involved a considerable sum of money, so it was worth considerable risk to acquire that money. The more important an official became, the more likely they would be corrupt simply because of the temptation from opportunities like this to acquire great wealth.

Romanus had much to gain from presenting his version of events in Africa, and he would take great care to conceal the benefits he would gain if his story was accepted as the truth. We, on the other hand, had little to gain except the restoration of the security our city had once known. Why was it so hard for the emperor to see what motivated people in this instance and thus know who was likely telling the truth and who was likely telling lies?

If the truth was that there had been no raids, then in fact we had nothing at all to gain and no reason to risk delivering the difficult message Jovinus delivered. That such self-evident facts as these could still be contested by further lies and allegations of other personal motives that were themselves highly improbable, spoke clearly enough about what the empire had become.

But Jovinus was still optimistic. He reminded me this inquest was an opportunity to irrefutably establish the truth of our claims. It could turn out well for us. There was much negotiating yet to come. This was the gamble we were taking; it was what we all committed to do on that day when everyone gathered in the basilica and debated our course of action. He assured me it was all for the best. I agreed with this and hoped his reasoning was sound.

We were now committed to delicate negotiations with powerful people who had the ability to help us or destroy us almost on a whim. The realization that we had to deal with imperial officials as if they were potential enemies was deeply unsettling. When a civilization can no longer channel the strivings of its powerful people into activities that support the greater good, then we are all in peril. When people cannot speak truth to power, when they must resort instead to wiles and flattery as the preferred method of communication, it becomes difficult if not impossible for most to prosper in such circumstances.

When honesty is discouraged, then lies fill in the gaps. Nobody knows who to trust. And without trust there is no unity, so everyone is vulnerable, even the most powerful.

Cordial Reception

We were instructed to return to Carthage and await the arrival of the emperor's envoy, Palladius. We had not met him during our time at court, but we knew of him and his reputation. His reputation was of the highest order. The emperor called him "incorruptible". We were encouraged by this. Perhaps our situation was not so dire after all.

Palladius was one of the emperor's inner circle, and his words would be accepted as truth by the emperor. In a further sign of the emperor's interest in the situation in Africa, Palladius was also entrusted with a large sum of money that he would deliver to the troops to pay them for wages that had fallen into arrears.

This time as we stepped off the ship that brought us back across the sea, Romanus himself was there to meet us at the docks. He was in a much more courteous mood than the one when we had last parted company. With him was a detachment of mounted soldiers and his own coach waited to take us and our luggage into the city. We made our way to army headquarters in the heart of the city across from the governor's palace. Romanus politely inquired about our journey and the sights we had seen while at court. What a change in his behavior I thought.

When we arrived at headquarters, we were told that arrangements had been made for us to stay at the governor's palace until Palladius arrived. That evening we were invited to dine with the governor and Romanus joined us. Again all was quite cordial. The governor himself had sent reports to Milan on the extent of the latest tribal raids. They were the topic of conversation as we ate. I felt much better. Jovinus was in a good mood. The food was well prepared.

Romanus took the opportunity to explain his side of the story to Jovinus and the governor. He explained his regret for the miscommunication that had occurred at our last meeting. The extra camels and provisions he requested were needed in order to support this army on a punitive campaign that likely called for an extended march into the desert. He emphasized that he completely understood the need to work with the city magistrates to determine an appropriate level of support for his campaign in light of the damage that the raids had already caused. It seemed something could be worked out.

A Man of Great Influence

It was good to be back in Africa. The weather was warmer every day and spring planting was happening everywhere. These rituals of spring connected me again with familiar patterns of life. A pleasant week was spent visiting friends and distant family members who lived in the city and on surrounding estates.

One afternoon upon returning from a visit to the estate of a distant cousin, we were informed that a ship from Ostia had arrived with the imperial envoy, and that he too was staying at the governor's palace. Dinner that night was a study in diplomacy, flattery and innuendo. The governor, Palladius, Romanus, Jovinus and I were joined by the vice governor and two other officials. Conversation was cheerful and carefully guarded.

I watched Palladius and attempted to use my new found worldliness learned at court to see what I could ascertain about who he might be. He was a tall and handsome man. His high cheekbones and light brown hair made him look to be a mix of Gothic and Pannonian blood. His Latin was good and he used classical analogies and allegories several times that night. His conversation was pleasant and I got the feeling he knew many things that he would never reveal except under dire torture.

In the morning a small convoy of wagons and coaches awaited us in the palace courtyard. We loaded ourselves and our luggage into one of the carriages. Palladius and his two assistants rode in a second coach. Following our coaches were several wagons loaded with provisions and heavy leather sacks of carefully counted coins. A detachment of cavalry wearing chain mail armor and carrying long swords and bows provided our escort.

After ruinous debasement of the currency caused by the endless civil wars of the military anarchy, the emperor Diocletian when he first restored order also overhauled the currency. He issued a coin that became the standard of value throughout the empire and beyond. That coin was the gold solidus containing a strictly regulated amount of gold and stamped with the emperor's bust on one side and an image of victory on the other. This was the coin that soldiers and merchants alike valued most. The bags were labeled with the names of the forts along the way where we would stop to deliver the soldier's pay.

Long gone where the big legionary bases from the time of Severus, the enemies of the empire had multiplied, and more soldiers were always needed but there were never enough. So a new strategy was devised. It was a strategy that called for smaller numbers of soldiers to be stationed at many strongly built little forts and castles. They had thick stone walls and high towers that enabled detachments of fifty or a hundred soldiers to hold out against many times that number of attacking barbarians who had limited capability for the siege warfare required to capture these strong points. In this way we protected roads, bridges and granaries where food was stored. Cities such as Leptis were surrounded by walls and had garrisons of troops to defend the walls. Those walls provided shelter for people and their animals and as many of their possessions as they could carry in times of danger.

With this strategy, raiders were denied easy movement along the roads, and the food and water needed to sustain them was out of easy reach behind strong walls. Swift horsemen and signal towers carried messages between the forts, and news of raids was quickly communicated to military headquarters. Well armed units of the mobile field army were then dispatched where needed to relieve besieged forts and cities. This system worked well as long as the soldiers got paid.

Over the next week as we made our way down the coast road from Carthage we stopped at forts and walled cities. Palladius was always received with ceremony. Garrisons turned out for our review, and honor guards escorted us from one stop to the next. Often commanding officers urged us to stay the night and provided us with comfortable sleeping accommodations and hearty meals.

As we left the following mornings, commanding officers always presented Palladius with gifts and their best wishes for a safe journey to the next stop. Palladius was a man of considerable influence who had the ear of the emperor. Gifts were common for people of such influence. How different the soldiers were when Palladius was present.

Palladius proceeded on to Leptis where a group of our more eloquent and distinguished citizens showed him everything, and told of the troubles they and their fellow citizens and had endured. Palladius toured and noted the burned estates, the wide swaths of cut down olive trees and the destruction of farm buildings and olive presses. He stayed in Leptis for several weeks gathering evidence and making notes. He was most kind and sympathetic to our plight.

By mid-summer he had seen enough and he and his entourage departed back to Carthage. We were pleased. Now our story would finally be told. The emperor would hear our plea and protect us.

Fragile Optimism

How could the emperor not fail to come to our aid and protect the green sea of olive trees that had taken hundreds of years to grow and which now supplied so much oil consumed by the empire? We knew we had powerful adversaries in Romanus and Remegius, but we believed we had a powerful ally in Palladius. We believed his integrity and the trust he had from the emperor would see us through and be our salvation.

Instead, we were taken completely by surprise. Just after the harvest was completed, a summons came by messenger. Jovinus was ordered to appear before a court of inquest in Carthage. The charge was treason for lying to the emperor. After seeing for himself the ashes and devastation visited upon our province by the raids, Palladius reported that there had been no raids. He reported that he had seen no destruction or damage to property. We were stunned. What happened?

Then I remembered how the money in the paymaster's wagons did not seem to dwindle that much as we made our way from one fort to another. I recalled the cheerful meetings Palladiaus had with different garrison commanders, and the happy partings on many mornings as we left one fort and proceeded to the next. Suddenly I understood.

In the following weeks we heard the details of what happened when Palladius returned to Carthage and confronted Romanus. At first Palladius was furious. He informed Romanus that the emperor would receive a full report of the extensive destruction he had seen. But Romanus was not worried.

Romanus had set a clever trap. He ordered the officers of the companies of soldiers we visited to hand back to Palladius half the pay he brought with him as a gift. Palladius was an influential man in close contact with the highest officials at court and with the emperor himself. This is how officers made connections and advanced their careers.

In their confrontation, Count Romanus assured Palladius the emperor would also receive a full report of how he, the incorruptible court official, had diverted to his own profit half of the money the emperor sent to pay the soldiers. At this point Palladius suddenly realized his predicament. And in light of this realization, he came to an understanding with Romanus.

In his report upon returning to the emperor's court, Palladius said the delegates from Leptis had spoken falsely. He reported that they had no cause for complaint. On hearing this, the emperor flew into a rage. As we knew, Valentinian was inclined to severity. And Remegius did nothing to distract or diminish his rage. He ordered Jovinus to be arrested and put on trial for treason. As his rage grew in intensity he ordered more and more people to be arrested and tried. He ordered me to be arrested. He even ordered the governor of Africa to be arrested since obviously the governor too had lied in his report of raids in the spring.

As arrests were made and confessions were extracted, more people were incriminated and further arrests were made.

Chapter 4

Embraced by an Angel

Two weeks after we heard of the emperor's decree, soldiers came to the door of our shipping office in the building near the harbor. The soldier in charge announced he was there to arrest Jovinus and take him to stand trial in Carthage. I stood between him and my uncle and demanded that he take me in his place. The soldier looked at me for a moment. He said nothing. Then he pushed me out of his way and proceeded to lay his hands on Jovinus. The other soldiers gathered around and escorted him to a wagon waiting outside.

Then Romanus sent his agents to Leptis to induce the families and the magistrates to make charges against Jovinus and denounce him for telling lies to the emperor. They made skillful use of bribes, blackmail and threats.

Deal with the Devil

And so it came to pass that the magistrates and leading families of Leptis positively declared they had given Jovinus no commission to report what he had reported to the emperor. "What can we do?" they asked each other. In the face of imperial wrath no one dared speak up.

Romanus saw his advantage and pressed it home. Through his agents he offered us all a deal. It had specially tailored features for each of us. For the magistrates, he said they shall be pardoned if they sign documents testifying that they did not approve Jovinus to take his message to the Emperor, and furthermore, state that Jovinus had told lies. For the families, he said all they need do was provide a few extra provisions and animals for the army. Or, if they wished, they could just provide him with cash payments if that was easier for them.

And for me and my family, he had a most special offer. It was known to everyone that the extremely likely outcome of the trial of Jovinus would be a disaster for the entire family. Jovinus would be found guilty and executed. And then the emperor would confiscate our family holdings and businesses. We would be lucky to be left with a single small farm for all of us to huddle together on and scratch out a living after that.

Romanus knew, as did we, that our only recourse was to transfer our property to the Christian church. That was the only way to shield it from confiscation. Then in return for this generous donation, the head of our family would be elected bishop, and thus it could be arranged for everyone to remain living on their estates and operating their businesses in the name of the church. After the execution of Jovinus, I would be the head of our family.

And there was something else. Because this transfer of property had become a common recourse for wealthy families in trouble, over the years it had steadily reduced the empire's tax base. So upon his ascension to power, Valentinian decreed a law that made it much harder for wealthy families to carry this out. Valentinian's new law said that if a wealthy man went into the church, then he must transfer his property to another relative who will remain outside the church. So the property would remain on the tax rolls, and remain subject to imperial confiscation.

We needed the help of Romanus and his friend the vice governor of Africa. And they were glad to help us for a fee equal to one quarter of our holdings. And in doing so, they also sealed our lips because if we should ever accuse them of corruption then we too would be exposed as having broken laws with serious consequences. That consummated our deal with the devil. We could never seek redress of our grievances.

Quite the opposite, we were now defenders of the devil to save our own skins.

I alone refused to accept this deal. I vowed to speak truth to power. This was more than I could bear. It was a choice I had never imagined I would have to make. I was numb.

Yet in meeting after meeting, magistrates and other noble families urged me to see reason. Do the right thing they said. Protect your family, your property, your city. See what happened to your uncle for speaking truth to power. This is a new time; we may still read the classics, but this is not a classical world. The other families assured me they could pay for the extra supplies required by Romanus without asking my family to contribute to that payment.

It was all inevitable. We had to merge our property with the church if we were to avoid having it confiscated. The charge for lying to the emperor is treason. Execution and confiscation are the penalties for treason. That is the law.

We sacrificed the head of our family and elevated me to the office of bishop in order to maintain the style of life we had long grown accustomed to; the style of life we were born into by fact of being a senatorial family. I knew the Christian stories well enough even then. I betrayed Jovinus just as Judas betrayed Jesus. And for my reward I became Bishop of Leptis to watch over my family wealth. I was paid far more than a mere 40 pieces of silver for my good deed.

We gave up Jovinus to save ourselves. The very person we proclaimed as our savior and sent forth as our spokesman, we now denied any knowledge of ever having asked such a thing, just as the disciples denied knowing Jesus in his final hours. All of us, the best families of Leptis, left him to his fate. Everyone told me to do what had to be done; for there was nothing that could be done to save Jovinus.

His trial was held and the sentence was carried out one morning in the autumn of that year 364. Each person, each family looked out for themselves as they felt they had to. The common good disappeared. Our world collapsed and we withdrew into ourselves.

The Brave Man Dies Only Once

How can I go on living with the knowledge of what I have done? With my final words to the agents of Romanus I conveyed our abandonment of Jovinus and sent him to his death. I betrayed my mentor and my dearest friend. My sorrow poured like torrents of grief from storm wracked mountain valleys.

In the days that followed, the families and magistrates of Leptis come to see me in my house by the theater to convey a message I had not expected. “That’s how life is,” they said with hopeless expressions as they shrugged their shoulders. “One has to do unpleasant things.” How did I not know this? What did I think we could do in the face of treachery from Romanus and the emperor’s rage? Speaking truth to that power was futile and suicidal.

They begged me to think of them and not further arouse the emperor’s anger. They told me I was a good and honest man, and that I had to save myself because they needed me. I was now first man of the city, and pillar of the church.

I cannot count the number of times I wished I could die after accepting that message.

On the morning of the day he was executed in Carthage, I was walking along the beach outside our city walls, lost in grief and shame. I was inconsolable and considered drowning myself in the sea. Then as I walked, there was a sudden commotion of seabirds calling and circling in the air above me.

I looked up to see a white mass of birds. Their shrill cries carried above the sound of the waves, and in the middle of that cloud of wings I saw something else. I swear I saw my uncle embraced by an angel.

Jovinus knew his duty and did it like a Roman. He saw how the game must end. He knew what he must do to salvage what could be salvaged. In the end, after a visit by Romanus, he signed his own confession of lying to the emperor in order seal the arrangements Romanus had made with us.

I heard this from Jovinus' wife when she returned from Carthage. She also delivered the letter he wrote to me on the morning of his execution. This is what he said:

> *The people of the city have turned into a panic stricken mob. Someone must stand firm to defend them until they recover their courage.*
>
> *I will stand and receive the wounds required to keep the enemy at bay while you Lucius must tear up the bridge to insure the enemy cannot cross.*
>
> *I will hold until I hear your shout. Then I will plunge into the river and emerge on the other side to be embraced and brought back into the city.*
>
> *When you read my letter say this prayer for me and for yourself –*
>
> > *Holy Father, I pray thee to receive into thy propitious stream these arms and this warrior.*

I knew exactly what he meant. He instructed me to do what had to be done to save the city. And he reminded me it was my turn now to stand on the bridge and hold the enemy at bay.

He used the allegory of Horatio on the bridge, the ancient Roman hero who saved the city of Rome from destruction by standing alone to defend the bridge into the city when its army fled in panic. Horatio told the fleeing soldiers to tear up the bridge behind him so the enemies of Rome could not cross the Tiber and destroy the city. The historian Livy tells us that though Horatio received grievous wounds, he held the enemy at bay until he heard the shout from the opposite bank that the bridge was down. Then he dove into the river after saying this prayer, “Holy Father, I pray thee to receive into thy propitious stream these arms and this warrior.”

I was overcome with remorse, but unlike Judas, I could not hang myself. It was my duty to live. I was the bishop. I led the people in their prayers for safety. I gave them back the hope and courage they gave up when they betrayed Jovinus. I gave them the forgiveness that Jovinus gave to me in his last letter.

A brave man dies just once, the fearful man dies many times. And perhaps a brave man does not die at all. Livy tells us Horatio did not die for his bravery. He did his duty, said his prayer, and dove into the water and swam back across the Tiber. He emerged on the other side with all his arms and armor intact, and was received with gratitude into the community he had defended with his bravery.

Did not Jovinus also defend us and dive into the water? Did I not see him emerge intact on the other side to be embraced and received by the community he defended with his bravery?

I took my place on the bridge. I struggled to do what had to be done to hold our enemies at bay. ∞

Memoirs of a Bishop

Emperor's Dream
on the Edge of the Desert

BOOK 3

Chapter 1

Coming Full Circle

IGITUR VERSO CIVITATIS STATU NIHIL USQUAM PRISCI ET INTEGRI MORIS

It was thus an altered world, and of the old unspoiled Roman character, not a trace lingered. - The Annals of Tacitus

It was as if the body of the empire feasted on itself. It came to be administered and defended by people who carelessly placed their own self-interest above that of the cities and the people under their care. Decay and collapse set in as wealth was drained from the provinces. The use of force to hold the empire together worked only to slow the collapse, but not to prevent it.

The land we had worked for centuries to reclaim from the desert became desert once more in large swaths where raiding tribes cut down the trees and destroyed the cisterns and irrigation works. And the raids killed many people so there were not enough farmers and peasants to tend the land and keep the irrigation works in good repair. Without the shade of the olive trees, the sun baked the ground, and as the soil lost its moisture it turned back to desert.

For eleven years we kept our silence. Romanus continued with his corrupt and extortionate ways over the provinces and cities he was appointed to protect. He acquired large sums of money. And finally the rapacity of Romanus and the greed and arrogance of his troops provoked rebellion in Africa. Valentinian sent another of his generals,

Count Theodosius, and a detachment of imperial troops to deal with the problem.

Romanus Revealed

Romanus brought ruin to everything he touched including himself. In his fixation on personal gain he never considered the effect of his actions on others; he simply did not feel it necessary; any more than he would have considered the effect of an order on one of his soldiers. Did he behave this way when he started out as a young man, or did he observe his superiors acting this way as he served them on his own rise through the ranks? This type of behavior became all too common in the army.

He was relieved of his command and placed under arrest. In going through the files and correspondence of Romanus, Count Theodosius discovered a letter sent to Romanus from an official at Valentinian's court that contained the following passage, "The disgraced Palladius sends you his greetings, and wishes you to know that the only reason for his disgrace was that in the affair of Tripolitania he uttered a lie to the sacred ear of majesty."

The letter was sent to court and there it was read. At long last, so many years after the events that irrevocably changed our lives, the corruption and lies of Romanus were revealed. Palladius was recalled from retirement to answer charges against him. He was under no illusions about what would happen, and one night on his journey back to court, while his guards were away, he hanged himself with his belt and thus embraced quickly his inevitable fate, and in this way avoided coming to that same fate after enduring far more pain for a much longer time.

Remegius had also left imperial service after amassing considerable wealth and arranging for a comfortable retirement. His former secretary at court was seized and put to torture to determine how much his former master knew of this affair. Upon hearing of this and fearing that his secretary would incriminate him, Remegius also hanged himself to escape the wrath of Valentinian.

Emperor Valentinian himself died soon afterward from a stroke which felled him during a fit of rage as he threatened and shouted at envoys from a troublesome tribe on the far side of the Danube. Valentinian's son became emperor. He pardoned Leptis and its citizens who were accused of treason. But the damage had been done. Leptis did not recover well from the raids and from its long years under official condemnation. Those events placed Leptis on a course that was hard to change.

Discerning Truth and Lies

Valentinian was the one most removed from events in Tripolitania, yet his decisions had the greatest effect. He depended on the reports of his envoys and petitions presented to him by his subjects to get the information he needed to make decisions. It was inevitable that those who wished to sway his decisions would lie to him or not reveal the entire truth. He and many rulers before him have often proved unable to discern between truth and lies, and the consequences have been severe.

There is a simple reality at work here. The more one person perceives another to be the source of something they want, the more time and effort that person will expend to convince the other person of the truth of the news they bring and the rightness of the requests they make. Emperor Valentinian was constantly assailed with news, flattery and requests. At times I find myself assailed with the same. I appreciate the inevitability of this condition.

The years of official disapproval and learning to survive in difficult situations taught me important lessons about truth and motivation. My survival then depended on learning these lessons well and remembering them once learned. I wish my tutors had taught me this in my days at school. I have made many mistakes and gone through much pain and confusion for lack of this knowledge.

I know I lack a quality Jovinus had in abundance which enabled him to see through people's tall tales and discern truth quickly. What he had, call it intuition; call it a merchant's cunning or a hunter's instinct; I do not have. To compensate, I strengthen what I do have. As the blind man develops other senses to compensate for his lack of sight, I have developed my intellect to compensate for my lack of intuition.

I have a thoughtful nature and am good at figuring out how things work. When I need to know about something whether it be how to plant and harvest wheat, or how to negotiate contracts for delivery of olive oil, I use my ability for finding the essential facts and seeing how they relate to each other. When I do this the big picture emerges. I see how the thing works and understand what to do.

But what I do now is not so easily defined. It is not always clear where one thing begins and another ends. I have to make decisions with far less understanding of essential facts, certainly when compared to my days of running our family estates or selling our oil. So I focus my intellect on detecting what is true. I try to see what is right in front of me and then use that truth to discover other related truths to guide me in the right direction.

Three Motives

With few exceptions, I find it fair to say that any subordinate who takes the risk of delivering bad news to a superior, or who delivers any message that is out of the ordinary, is animated by one of three motives. The first of these three motives is fear or urgent necessity. The second one is strong belief in the message. And the third motive is a scheme to gain some benefit. I find those who operate from the third motive are the most numerous. They may be subordinates or anyone else who comes my way.

Good news makes me happy, yet it is in the bad news or unexpected news that I find most opportunities to either avoid misfortune or reap an additional harvest. As a consequence, I pay particular attention to this type of news and to those who deliver it.

I can recognize someone driven by the first motive – urgent necessity – by noting the level of fear or excitement in their voice and their face. Reports delivered by people driven by this motive are not lies. People driven by this motive are telling the truth as they perceive it to be. What I need to assess is the likelihood that such a person actually knows what they are talking about, or if they have only a partial understanding.

The second motive for telling bad or unexpected news comes from some strong belief in the person delivering this news. I determine the likelihood of this motive by assessing a person's degree of conviction. Those driven by this second motive have a certainty and self-assurance about them that is at times even exasperating. News delivered by such a parson is reliable to the extent that such a person is wise enough to recognize what is true and what is false. That wisdom is what I assess. News from someone who believes strongly in things that are not true is news that is useless or worse.

This brings me to the third motive – schemes to gain benefits. This is the motive that most often animates subordinates and others whom I meet. This motive can sometimes be confused with the motive of strong belief, but upon closer examination I find this third motive lacks the depth and certainty that is the hallmark of the second motive. There is intensity in this third motive, but it is a narrow and selfish intensity. It does not match the intensity that comes from belief in a cause or a project that is truly greater than oneself.

When evaluating information delivered by someone with this third motive; experience teaches me time and again how important it is to find out the size and likelihood of that person's potential gain. While asking questions, I watch to see how forthcoming that person is in revealing such information. The less forthcoming a person is, the less I trust the information they provide.

Opportunity and Misfortune

Of those who are forthcoming, I still consider how their potential gains shape their presentation of the facts. It is indeed this group of people with whom I spend much of my time. Groups of relatively forthcoming people who want something from me, and who can do something in return, are people I want to associate with. Such people make good business connections. These groups are where I find opportunity.

I have learned that dark and uneasy groups are often dominated by people who speak from the second motive yet do not have the ability to distinguish between what is true and what is rumor and superstition. Their insistent pushing of falsehoods creates in them an angry and defensive behavior. They become dismissive of all who do not agree with them. It is as if they are in some way aware of their own foolishness, and are bracing themselves for the inevitable collapse that eventually accompanies all untenable positions. Followers and hangers on in these groups are swayed by the opinions of the leaders and often driven by the first motive, in the form of fear for their safety or an urgent greed to acquire something otherwise out of their reach.

Many groups are dominated by those who speak from the third motive and cleverly hide their potential gains with lies and partial truths. They know quite well what they are doing. They go to great lengths to appear uninterested in personal gain. Religious and political settings are where I often find people of this sort. I have learned to watch for them. It is a ceaseless task to avoid being fooled by the skills of these people.

Unavoidable Consequences

Although our family had merged its property with the church and I had become the bishop of Leptis, there were nonetheless other issues that could not be avoided. In the years after the execution of Jovinus our family and other noble families of Leptis were ostracized by the imperial administration and by the business networks we had so long been a part of.

We found it exceedingly difficult to win new contracts to supply the annona in Rome. We found the noble families of other cities far less interested in dining with us or inviting us to dine with them. We found it best to arrange for a go-between to be the official seller of record on the contracts we did get. We found it wise to restrict our participation in the social life of Carthage, Rome and Milan.

It came as a deep sadness to realize we no longer had a place of honor in the world. Our family had known honor and respect in the highest circles since the reign of Severus. We could not at first believe it had changed; it happened so quickly. It took us all by unhappy surprise.

And because we no longer enjoyed respect in the highest circles, we no longer knew what was happening. We were reduced to the embarrassing position of begging for scraps of information that were often revealed too late for us to capitalize on anyway. It was not possible to continue doing business in such a position as that.

Nonetheless, it was our determination to rebuild. That meant we had to turn our attention away from the west and look to the east. The empire was in many respects now two different kingdoms, the provinces of the west and the provinces of the east. Though in theory both were united in the eternal Roman Empire, in practice both had their own administrators, and their own armies, and their own emperors who were of equal rank with each other. Each was a sovereign entity onto itself. Leptis in the province of Tripolitania was officially part of the western empire, but our future now lay in the eastern empire.

Once this decision was made, uncle Victorinus sold the villa Septimi outside Rome and wrapped up our business operations there. He took his family east to a similar villa outside Constantinople on the shores of the Bosporus. The cultivation of relationships with important people in charge of procuring the food supply for Constantinople became his new focus.

The other important city for the family was Alexandria. Where Carthage in the west was no longer so welcoming to us, we turned east to Alexandria. Alexandria and Egypt, with the provinces of Palestine and Syria, were much involved in the trade networks that centered on Constantinople. That was where we needed to go to replace business we were losing in the western empire.

In an area near the harbor in Alexandria we established a sizable warehouse for selling olive oil and other products from Leptis. Soon I began spending much of my time there making contacts and transacting business.

Alexandria was a different, and perhaps more worldly city than Carthage. Its streets were busy and its people were outspoken. Combined with this outspoken nature was the inquiring and thoughtful nature of the Greek philosophers and teachers who so greatly influenced the city's culture. The greatest library in the world was in Alexandria, and many people came there to learn.

Chapter 2

The Gospel of Thomas

That autumn in the year 384 as I left Leptis and returned to Alexandria I was losing my will to continue. Even though the emperor had pardoned us, and the citizens of Leptis gave me their respect, it left me feeling empty and lonely. I was stalked by feelings of despair which increasingly consumed my ability to concentrate.

My situation seemed hopeless. I left Leptis after the harvest that year knowing how much wheat and olive oil we needed to sell in Alexandria. I began calling on buyers. Prices were down and business was hard. It seemed nothing could be done beyond a stubborn defense of what we had salvaged from those events of twenty years prior, and even that was slipping away a bit more each year.

This was not the life I wanted for myself. I was not the man I wanted to become when I accompanied Jovinus on his mission to speak truth to power. On that journey I faced my fears of the deep and the world beyond. My feelings of inadequacy gave way to confidence as I found my way. I thought I might someday become head of the family for my resourcefulness and perseverance, not just by circumstances of my birth.

Then, beyond anything I could have imagined, those dreams were shattered. Regardless of what others did and said, regardless of what they implored me to do, I knew then, and every year thereafter, my actions were neither honorable nor brave. It was my place to stand with

Jovinus. And if that meant death then so be it. I abandoned him instead. And for my cowardice, I was made bishop of Leptis. I accepted worldly gain and turned away from the very virtues I now presumed to represent and teach to others. My shame was overpowering.

I found little joy and no self-respect in my life after that. There were many reasons for doing what I did, and many clever arguments had been made to justify my actions. But there is a point where reasons and arguments are no longer enough. There is a point where one cannot avoid coming to terms with one's beliefs and one's actions and addressing the tensions that arise between the two. Once this point is reached, further delay is fatal, both to the mind and to the body. I was at that point. I did not know what to do next.

Bookseller Street in Alexandria

One of the main streets that lead from the piazza in front of the Library in Alexandria is the street where booksellers have their shops. This cobblestone street is lined with sturdy stone buildings three and four stories high. On the first floors facing the street are shops where books and scrolls can be examined and purchased. Because of its reputation, books and buyers from far off and exotic places find their way to Alexandria.

One evening I came across such a book and found myself to be a buyer. I was heading home from our warehouse near the harbor. As I came to the Library and crossed the piazza, I strolled down the street of the booksellers. It was early evening in the summer and still light out. A cool breeze off the sea was blowing into the city and it flowed up the street from the harbor.

Merchants were sitting on chairs outside their shops and some exhibited their prize merchandise to attract attention from passersby like myself. It was pleasant with that cool breeze and the reddish evening light. Street lamps were just being lit. Lamps and candles lighting the insides of shops could be seen through their windows and doors.

After a few minutes as I walked along the street, I looked over to my left and met the smile of a bookseller sitting outside his shop. On a table next to him was a magnificent leather bound book with gold lettering and designs on the front cover. He caught my eye and smiled, his hand swept over the book. I smiled back and walked toward him.

How could one not at least glance at such a splendid book? He greeted me in broken Latin with a strong Greek accent. My Greek was not what it should have been after all my schooling, but then we never spoke Greek in Leptis or Carthage, so much of my Greek had been forgotten. Alexandria however spoke Greek as its primary language, Latin was second. We exchanged greetings and again he motioned me to examine the book. As I opened the cover and scanned the pages, he went inside his shop.

The book was written in Latin in a neat and steady hand. It was a collection of stories and poetry from Roman authors of the Antonine Age; those writers of the words that will forever be associated with the peak of the Roman world, authors such as Virgil, Ovid, Horace and Cicero. As I read their words it produced a deep sadness in me. These were words I had read many times in my years of education by tutors in my home and by philosophers in the forum. These were classical words but this was no longer a classical world.

I looked up to see the bookseller offering me a cup of saffron tea. The saffron smell is common in Alexandria and I find it quite inviting. This spice comes from India and Persia. Merchants bring it up the Red Sea and then overland to Alexandria to be shipped on to the rest of the empire. I was lost in my thoughts and thanked him as I took the cup. He smiled and stepped back as I sipped the tea.

It was getting darker and stores along the street were starting to close. It suddenly occurred to me that by accepting his cup of tea I had entered into the Alexandrian convention which meant I would stay longer at his store and most probably buy something. I did not want to keep him waiting any longer, and it would soon be too dark to see much anyway. This gold lettered book was not what I was looking for. So I stepped inside his shop. The walls were covered with shelves of books and scrolls. Absently I walked to one of the shelves and pulled down a slim collection of paprus pages bound in a simple leather cover. On the cover Greek letters in black ink said, *The Gospel According to Didymos Judas Thomas*.

I flipped the book open. It was a collection of sayings. They were written in Greek on the left side page and in Egyptian Coptic on the right side page. My understanding of written Greek was better than my ability with the spoken word, and these visits to Alexandria were bringing back my command of the language. I scanned some of the sayings, piecing together approximate translations from what I could understand. Some of these sayings were familiar, some I had never heard before. Yet what I read spoke directly and without preamble. The sayings asked rhetorical questions and made statements with a blunt authority, as if their truth was obvious for those who could see. As if the truth was right in front of my face, and all I needed to do was recognize it.

I looked over at the bookseller and held up the book. He smiled. He took it and looked it over and quoted a price. It was the end of the day and instead of bargaining over the price I just gave him what he asked and shook his hand, and hurried on up the street to the house where I stayed during my trips to Alexandria.

According to Thomas, Who Doubted

That night in my lodgings, I opened the book and read those sayings. There are only 114 of them. They are said to be the sayings of Jesus as they were remembered and written down by his disciple Thomas. I was a bishop and I knew about this Thomas. He was the disciple who when told of Jesus' resurrection, announced he did not believe it. He said he would need to see Jesus alive with his own eyes and touch the spear wound in his side to verify that this was Jesus and he was alive again.

Thomas did see the resurrected Jesus, and he did touch the wound in his side. This evidence changed his mind. It convinced him death can indeed be overcome. After this, Thomas went to Alexandria and made his way down the Nile to a village where he spent some years living with a small community of followers. There he wrote down the sayings of Jesus as he remembered them. Then he alone among the disciples left the empire and traveled east to spread the teachings beyond the Roman world. It was said by some that he was the twin brother of Jesus. In Greek his name Didymos means twin and in Aramaic his name Thomas also means twin.

He took passage on a merchant ship from the ancient city of Berenice and traveled down the Red Sea and across to India where he founded a church in one of the rich trading cities on the coast there. It was said a thriving community grew around his teachings, and in his seventy second year he died from a spear wound to his side delivered by a soldier in that city.

The book in my hands began with the statement, "*These are the secret sayings which the living Jesus spoke and which Didymos Judas Thomas wrote down.*" In the tone of voice that came through as I read the words that followed, it seemed to me this person was speaking truth to power. Difficult messages were delivered to people who wanted to hear other things. And in this case the speaker is the subordinate, because he knows his words must be heard and acted upon by the reader if his wish is to be fulfilled.

The reader was the powerful one, it was the reader's decision to accept or ignore these words. If the reader or listener did not accept the words then the speaker would die with his words. It seemed to me the speaker was both Jesus and Thomas. They were words of Jesus but they were presented by Thomas in his own way. Where other disciples took care to tell stories that entertained the reader and further explained the words, Thomas dispensed with those embellishments. Where other disciples said the Kingdom will come, Thomas said the Kingdom was already here for those who could see it.

As I read the sayings that followed, it became clear they were meant not so much as literal statements, but as symbolic and figurative statements that pointed to the answer, but did not attempt to literally spell out the answer. They called upon the reader to make that final, uniquely personal discovery on their own.

I had become bishop under questionable circumstances, yet I was nonetheless a bishop and I had a sincere desire to do well. In my sermons I repeated the accepted teachings of the church, but found the dogma to be simple and predictable. In his gospel Thomas took a different approach. Because Thomas was a doubter and a skeptic and a wanderer, it made me all the more interested in his book.

I knew also that this gospel had been banned. By the will of the Emperor Constantine, who wanted an end to Christian squabbling and an orthodoxy which all could understand and adhere to, the First Council of Nicaea was convened in 325, and among other things, it declared the Gospel of Thomas to be heresy. It was decreed that these words were troubling and confusing to the faithful. All copies of this gospel were ordered to be burned.

For the most part, this edict was obeyed. And for those who did not obey, it confirmed their belief in the essential truth of this gospel. For what other reason could such sayings be banned except for the consequences of speaking truth to power?

Interpretation of These Sayings

I saw in these sayings that Thomas wrote down unmistakable signs of speaking truth to power. I could see no reason for the speaker to present these messages other than his belief in their truth. Acceptance of these statements would not increase the personal power of the speaker because they directed the reader to look to themselves instead. This speaker spoke from the second motive. The question for me to assess was how knowledgeable was this person on the subject that he spoke about.

The first saying in the book announced,

> *"And He said, 'Whoever finds the interpretation of these sayings will not experience death.'"*

The next saying spoke directly to the situation I found myself in. It did not attempt to either encourage me with good news or hide the difficulty of the work yet to be done. But then I did not want false encouragement. What I wanted was credible insight to help me determine if my labors were worthwhile and if I was on the right path. The second saying was,

> *"Let him who seeks continue seeking until he finds. When he finds, he will become troubled. When he becomes troubled, he will be astonished, and he will rule over the All."*

Instead of expecting people to blindly follow the interpretations of their bishops, the sayings directed people to look inside themselves for answers because that is where insight and knowledge resides. The words used depended on their inherent truth to make themselves self-evident. They deliberately used dualistic images that pushed the reader to transcend literalism and grasp the symbolic meaning that occurs when those dualistic images are merged. The third saying was this:

> *"If those who lead you say, 'See, the Kingdom is in the sky,' then the birds of the sky will precede you. If they say to you, 'It is in the sea,' then the fish will precede you. Rather, the Kingdom is inside of you, and it is outside of you. When you come to know yourselves, then you will become known, and you will realize that it is you who are the sons of the living Father. But if you will not know*

> *yourselves, you dwell in poverty and it is you who are that poverty."*

As I read those words that night, the eternal Roman world had been coming apart for decades; tribes and enemies on many frontiers raided our cities and laid waste our lands. Yet it seemed the best minds of the empire were paying no attention. Instead, they were embroiled in bitter controversy over the literal meanings of the words of Jesus. There were many conflicting Christian factions, and each had their own particular interpretations. They jostled each other for power and influence with increasing vehemence. In addition to the members of the imperial Orthodox Church, there were large numbers of other Christians who belonged to sects such as Arians, Monophysites, and Donatists to name just a few. Each of these congregations followed the teachings of their bishops, and they proclaimed the interpretations of their bishops to be the only true interpretations.

Because the empire's troubles were so overwhelming, and because most Roman citizens were so powerless to respond in any meaningful way, much energy was devoted instead to teaching and debating the words of Jesus. These words were explained in ever more literal ways so as to reach an ever wider audience. And in those increasingly literal interpretations there was less and less room for acceptance of other interpretations that did not agree on the particulars and the minutia.

Each detail of interpretation became divine magic; part of a complex collection of symbols and rituals required to gain the favor of the Almighty. All eternity was at stake in determining the correctness of these interpretations, and because the stakes were so high, the adherents of each faction clung stubbornly and fearfully to their particular interpretations.

After Emperor Constantine convened the first ecumenical council other emperors convened other councils. The purpose of those councils was always the same, to reconcile arguments over the details of the minutia related to different interpretations of the words. Emperor Constantine turned to Christianity as a way to unite the different peoples and cities of the empire, so he and the emperors who followed did not care about the minutia. They only wanted agreement and unity.

But many bishops did care about the minutia. Many of these bishops acted from the third motive; they told big stories for big personal gains in which they always professed not to be interested. As large numbers of followers accepted their interpretations of the minutia it made them powerful, and give them control, if not ownership, of much wealth as they rose in the Church.

It seemed to me then as it seems to me now, the only possible way out of such endless arguing is to stop attempting to reduce the words to literal statements. Each person must find their own version of the truth contained in the words, and in so doing, must see that this truth transcends any particular collection of words or minutia.

> *"He who will drink from my mouth will become like Me. I myself shall become he, and the things that are hidden will become revealed to him." Saying #108*

The Desert Fathers

One of my customers in Alexandria was a member of a prosperous merchant family. He was educated by teachers in Alexandria and finished his education in Constantinople. He briefly studied law in Beirut, and then returned to work in his family business. We had much in common he and I, and I instinctively liked him upon our first meeting. Aurelius Felix was his name.

Although I did not speak with him about it directly, Felix was able to see my personal anguish well enough. He sensed my sadness and despair. He often invited me to dine with him and his wife and their extended, noisy family of cousins and uncles and grand mothers. I accepted his invitations gladly. Their house was in a pleasant neighborhood east of the harbor and near enough to the shore to hear the sound of the waves on many nights.

Four generations lived in a sprawling two story structure that combined elements of a common city apartment block and a Roman villa. Sometimes the combination was jarring in its lack of refinement, such as the awkward placement of their dining room in relation to the peristyle garden. The view into the garden was not at all correct, and no Roman of noble family would have tolerated that clumsiness for fear of being mocked behind his back by his noble peers. The Aurelius family was descended from freed slaves and had done well as merchants. They did not care what noble families said about them behind their backs.

Dinners were filled with talk about nothing in particular, and yet our talk was somehow light hearted without being forced. There was a sense that anything could be said and nothing could be so bad given that we were all together, drinking wine, sharing food and enjoying each other's company. Those dinners were like coming to a green oasis after days in the desert. I began to live from one to another, always looking forward to the next.

One evening at dinner Felix said to me, "I think you would like a visit to Scetis." He looked at me and continued, "It is one of the communities in the western desert. Many go there to gain knowledge and find answers to their questions."

"Why do you mention this to me?" I asked with a certain forced smile.

He raised an eyebrow and smiled back at me. "Do I have to tell you stories and entertain you?"

I knew what he meant. I had spoken to him on previous occasions about finding the book of sayings written down by Thomas. I had spoken to him of my respect for the forthright delivery of difficult messages, and the way Thomas had dispensed with entertaining stories in favor of blunt words.

Felix said, "I have gone there myself. I stayed for some time and addressed issues that needed to be addressed. I can take you there. You will see, joining a community of others who seek answers to questions similar to yours will speed you on your journey."

He concluded by saying, "You need to go. And I think you need to go now." Without further argument I accepted the obvious veracity of what he said.

The next morning I told my nephew who assisted me with our warehouse in Alexandria that he was now in charge. When he asked me what that meant, I told him it meant I believed he was ready for this opportunity to grow his stature and responsibility in the family business. When he gave me a puzzled look in response, I told him I was going to be away on urgent business. He asked me how long and I said I did not know, perhaps a year, perhaps longer. I gave him a letter I had written to the family in Leptis and entrusted it to his care for delivery. I assured him it would be his time of good fortune, and that the family would send additional help if he requested it. I think he was beginning to warm to the prospect as I walked out the door. In any case, it was no longer my problem. I now had bigger issues to wrestle with.

I had to reconcile myself to the things I had done, or I could not go on. Many such as I had retired to the spiritual communities of the desert to find guidance and do battle with daemons within and without that threatened to destroy us. In the Egyptian desert west of the Nile delta were three communities of spiritual learning. They were Nitria, Scetis and Kellia. Felix told me bluntly, "Scetis is the one for you, the one the Coptic monks call Skete."

Beyond Literal Interpretations

A group of desert fathers and the brothers who lived in their houses at Skete pursued a program of work and study, quietly guided by the Gospel of Thomas. In their study, they were influenced by the writings of the learned Origen who strongly deplored literal interpretations of the words of Jesus. Origen wrote of the great divide between the masses who are capable of understanding only literal descriptions from the world of the senses, and those who have made their journey of personal discovery, those who can contemplate the non-literal and dualistic meaning of scripture and its otherwise impenetrable mysteries.

In the deafening silence and remorseless presence of the desert, I found mentors who had spent decades contemplating the transcendent meaning of the 114 sayings. The study of those blunt, unadorned words and their deliberately dualistic and difficult imagery would, they believed, bring forth into the world the light of grace. It would enable one to grasp the mysteries of the non-literal and dualistic nature of opposites, and the endless ways in which they combine to create the living divinity in us all, a divinity which is possessed of transcendent qualities not seen individually in any of its parts.

I entered into community with brothers who devoted their lives, for the time they were there, to the contemplation of these sayings and the attainment of self-awareness. We lived in houses of 12 brothers each. We worked on common projects to sustain our house, and we took breakfasts and dinners together. Every Sunday all the many houses of brothers and sisters in the community came together for services in the big basilica churches of Skete.

We were encouraged to touch the wounds we bore, and understand why they caused us such pain.

> *His disciples said, "When will You become revealed to us and when shall we see You?"*
>
> *Jesus said, "When you disrobe without being ashamed and take up your garments and place them under your feet like little children and tread on them, then will you see the Son of the Living One, and you will not be afraid" Saying #37*

I could not disrobe without shame. I could not lay bare my body because the wound inflicted on me had not healed. I covered this ulcerating wound because I feared what I might see if I looked upon it, and what others might say if they beheld it. I could not tread on my garments like a child because I did not have the self-awareness or presence in the moment that is had by a child. My wound distracted me with pain; it confined me with shame; it restrained me from joyful participation. I could not see the truth that was right before my eyes.

At times we were encouraged to retire alone deep into the desert to seek out our personal truths. Our resolve was tested by encounters with daemons that we found there. If one of us did not return from his journey within a period of time agreed to by the fathers, then his brothers would go in search of him.

There were solitary cells for such solo journeys built far out in the desert many years ago by those who came before. If a person was in one of those places he could be found and brought back. But if his journey and his daemon had taken him beyond those places, then most likely, he would not be found. Such was the nature of these journeys.

Sunlight, Solitude and Spiritual Guidance

After some months at Skete spent in spiritual study and learning the ways of survival in this place, the desert fathers encouraged me to confront my personal daemon. They could see my daemon was consuming me. I too realized that if I did not do battle with this daemon and emerge victorious, I would inevitably loose my will to live. There was no escaping; there was no other path.

My daemon provided me with a way cope, but it diverted me from addressing the causes of my pain. My daemon offered me a deceptively simple solution, and it seemed at the time to be the only practical solution. In the years since those events culminating in the death of Jovinus, I tried hard to forget and turn my thoughts to other things. What else was I to do?

I adopted an attitude of studied indifference. The very responses of the families of Leptis which resulted in my elevation to bishop were born of an indifference that manifested itself in hopeless shrugs and resigned sighs. The excuses we told ourselves about doing what we must do in order to survive were themselves a part of that indifference. By adopting this indifference I gave my daemon entry to my house. I allowed the daemon to enter because it provided me with the numbing sensation I needed to keep my feelings at bay, and keep my thoughts from straying into places I could not bear to go.

Yet the price this daemon extracted as time went on was draining me of my strength and resolve. And still underneath this dearly bought layer of feigned indifference, the sadness and emptiness born of those events from years ago only grew larger. Each year I slipped further into that emptiness and despair. It could not continue.

Clad in my monk's cloak, robe and sandals, I set off one summer morning well before sunrise. Slung across my chest and over one shoulder was the strap of a leather bag hanging at my side. It contained two flasks of water, sweet dates, some almonds, olive oil, a small bag of salt, and two loafs of bread. In a separate pocket of this bag was my book with the 114 sayings. I wished to be far into the desert before the first obstacles on my journey challenged me and tried to dissuade me from going further.

Daemons have their agents who can turn away all but the most committed travelers. And the more powerful the daemon, the more powerful are their agents. The merciless sun of the western desert in the summer time can be such an agent. It possesses a depth and intensity like few others.

My plan was to reach a certain cell built by a brother who had retired there some hundred and eighty years ago to escape the persecutions that occurred under the reign of my ancestor Severus. He and many others in that time found, somewhat to their surprise, that the predictable sequence of events that plays out in the desert from one sunrise to the next has great potential to create self-awareness. This predictability, and the lack of other distractions, focuses the mind. And in this process the mind is guided by the relentless nature of the desert which demands disciplined action and clear thinking in order to survive.

The desert fathers gave me a map and directions to follow so that I might find my way to this solo cell. It would be my home in which to receive a visit from my daemon. It was best if I reached that home before the third sunrise. It would, in fact, be an indication that I was lost if I did not arrive before the third sunrise. And the implications of being lost in such a land were, of course, severe.

As that first day wore on, I found exasperating omissions and ambiguities in the map and directions. My anger and indignation combined with the heat and sunlight of the desert to distract, confuse and intimidate me. Confidence in my ability to see clearly and make good decisions was tested from one moment to the next. The heat became impossible. Fears of what could happen undermined my courage.

My studies and training taught me it was essential to rise above the fears that shimmered all around me in the hot desert air. Survival meant engaging this world with my body and senses, and observing this world with my mind and intuition. In this state of awareness I could learn the lessons that my actions revealed. Engagement with the world is movement; observation is repose. Through movement and repose I would discover what I needed in order to find my way through the burning land.

At times I saw glimpses of my daemon. In sidelong glances I a caught momentary sight of its grinning face. It found me amusing. It emerged from behind shimmering curtains of blazing heat and disappeared again. Illusions ranging from obvious forgeries like pools of water glimmering in the distance, to temporarily convincing images of strange towers and approaching riders were thrown in my path to confuse and lure me. Conflict created by the different messages of my bodily senses and my lucid observations gave way as the day wore on to silence, and then to a growing awareness of a second presence. I became aware of someone who was both having the experience and observing the experience at the same time.

The first day ended as I traversed the sandy floor of a long desert valley with steep rocky outcrops on either side. The walls of the valley turned a golden color that shaded into orange and red as the sun set. Then slowly they turned to shades of purple, and suddenly, it was dark. In that darkness I stopped where I found myself. I went down on one knee as I had done many years ago in the presence of the emperor. Reaching into my bag, I broke off a piece of bread. I dripped a little olive oil on it and took a sip of water to moisten my lips. I put the bread in my mouth and chewed slowly, then washed it down with another sip of water. I ate a few dates. I sat quietly and waited. Maybe I even dozed for a few moments.

When I opened my eyes again, it was time to continue on my way.

The moon was rising. It was almost full. This had figured prominently in the timing of my journey. The light of this moon called a hunter's moon enabled me to continue through the cooler air of the night. The landscape was colored in shades of grey running from almost white to deepest black. I could see the land and find my way. As I walked, the moonlight brought back memories of the Villa Selene, and those many nights growing up when I felt the moon as a benevolent and protective presence watching over me.

By early afternoon on the second day, I spotted in the distance the landmark that was the beacon for my destination. The heat was intolerable, but I allowed myself to feel an almost smug satisfaction at seeing through the illusions thrown at me, and persevering along what had proven to be the right course. However, the desert has many ways of deceiving travelers, and making landmarks seem closer than they really are is one of those ways.

As the afternoon faded into evening, I continued on toward my destination without seeming to make much progress for all my walking. My smug satisfaction gave way to irrational fear, one emotion swung over to its opposite. Why was I not there already? What was taking so long? Was this landmark an illusion? Was it best to turn back now while there was still time?

There was nothing to be done except endure my fears in as much silence as could be mustered; these fears were the agents of the daemon. They were sent to wear me down and deter me from further efforts to confront that daemon. Resistance and arguing only goads these agents to redouble their efforts. I learned to use the very difficulties of the desert itself to focus my mind on more important matters, and thus allow me to ignore those endless nagging fears.

I came to my solo cell as the last sunlight of the second day was fading. It was a cave high on a hill under a rocky outcrop overlooking an endless expanse of desert dotted here and there with other rocky hills and outcrops. The mouth of the cave was enclosed by a wall made of rocks collected from the surrounding hillside. There was a single small doorway to provide entry and let in light. Otherwise, because of careful placement of the rocks and occasional sculpting of rocks to fit a particular niche, the wall was sturdy and solid. It kept out the wind and sand, and shielded the cave from the occasional cloudbursts of driving rain that came during certain times of the year.

Inside, the cave had been somewhat squared and straightened by placement of other carefully fitted rock walls. There was a sleeping bench made of fitted rocks and a small shrine likewise built, with an unadorned wooden cross fixed to the wall above it. The floor was flagstone and the ceiling was the ceiling of the cave itself. Two rocks the size of a hand jutted out from the wall opposite the sleeping bench offering places to hang my bag and my cloak.

I ate a handful of figs and washed them down with a few gulps of water. In the last evening light I read a saying from my book that seemed most relevant. Then I lay down on the sleeping platform and rolled up in my cloak. I was grateful for the exhaustion brought on by the rigors of the trip as it let me fall asleep quickly. Several times I awoke during the night. Looking down the length of my sleeping platform, past my feet and through the open door, hundreds of brilliant stars in the clear night sky made the outline of the door easy to see. Against that backdrop I awoke once to see the shape of a scorpion with its claws out in front and its tail and sharp stinger curled forward over its moving body. In times like this danger is real, but fear is only a distraction from the movement of either crushing the creature, or sweeping it quickly out the door. I did the latter.

Days followed each other in a predictable sequence. The regularity of each day freed me from distractions and the severe discipline required of me to face each day focused my mind. The heat even within the shade of my cell became considerable as the day progressed. And emerging from this shade into the blinding sunlight was necessary from time to time to cut through the hopeless confusion of conflicting thoughts that accumulated in my head.

Sunlight could clear my mind, but letting sunlight overpower me meant death. Food and water sustained me, but drinking more water than the day's few allotted sips or eating more than the day's handful of dates and almonds or mouthful of bread was dangerous. This was the severe discipline that guided my movement and my repose.

Time grew still. I awoke to find myself at different moments, sometimes in sunlight, sometimes in star light. I found a rhythm. I felt the steady presence of one who experiences and observes; one who exists in the consciousness that arises in the tension between light and dark, between movement and repose.

Blessed are the Solitary and Elect

But still I had seen only a few fleeting glimpses of the daemon I came so far to confront. This daemon did not yet take me seriously; it saw no reason to worry. When my allotted time was up and my journey was over, I would return to where I started, and be still a dependable devotee of this daemon. The very skills and discipline that had gotten me this far would soon become the daemon's best assurance that they also would prevent me from going any farther.

As my day to return arrived, I had not received the visit I sought. This presented me with two questions, and only two questions. First, was I truly in the presence of one who both experiences and observes? And second, did I desire my daemon's visit enough to trust completely in that presence? The contemplation of these two questions overcame me. My mind went blank.

I found myself standing naked one morning on my robe in the middle of my cell looking toward the door. On checking my supply of water and food, I saw both were almost gone, and realized the peril in which I had placed myself. I determined it to be several days beyond my appointed time to return. Whether I did so consciously or not, I had taken a dangerous path that depended on my connection with the presence I claimed to feel if I was going to survive. This realization washed over me in the slow, fluid way that defines the movement of time in places such as this. On looking toward the door I saw the shimmering wall of sunlight outside.

Then a shadow fell across that blaze of light. My daemon had arrived.

The daemon was cordial. Its presence brought relief to my eyes from the relentless sunlight as it stood there in the doorway. I picked up my robe and placed it on the bench and sat down. I crossed my legs in front of me and my back was straight. The daemon had a bald head and an orange beak with a circle of dark feathers starting at the base of its neck. I thought of a vulture. It cocked its head and arched a brow over one of its big yellow eyes.

I nodded my head, and it entered my cell. I saw a vision of myself as I was in that moment, sitting cross legged with eyes closed on my robe in the middle of my sleeping platform. Then I saw this vision extend to an endless number of me sitting cross legged on our robes in a line that receded off to the distant horizon of a desert landscape lit by the light of a setting sun.

Into my head there came an insistent question, "Who cares?" All of the instances of me extending to the horizon asked this question in unison and then repeated it. I knew I had to answer, and I knew this was no time for flippancy or clever evasions. The answer was beyond words. And depending on the answer, I either would or would not come back from this journey. I hesitated. The question continued to repeat over and over. I felt an urgent need to say something; my answer could not be delayed much longer.

I wanted to say the right thing. Part of me had an answer, yet I also knew it was only as an intellectual abstraction; a safe, predictable collection of words without real substance. It would do me no good in this situation. Again I hesitated. But the question did not stop.

The daemon had come to collect. For years it had helped me cope with my dilemma and provided excuses for my actions. It gave me the numbing drug of indifference. Now it ordered me to give my soul into its keeping as payment for further deliveries of this drug.

Unlike the distracting agents of fear sent to bother me with their endless questions that preyed on my self-doubt, this daemon could not be ignored. Though phrased as a question, what I heard was not a question, it was a demand. It bore down on me. I drew myself up for battle. I shouted back. I quoted scripture. I hurled abuse. My daemon came closer; it fed on my resistance. In the presence of my anger it grew even more ferocious. It crowded up close to me. It mocked me; it called me out; it demanded payment.

In that moment when there is nothing left to say or do, when the battle has already been won or lost, the answer appears. It is a dangerous moment because there is no further struggle or feat of arms that could save me if my answer proved inadequate. Yet my actions and observations up to that moment had already determined the outcome. And that outcome would now be revealed to me.

The sneering, mocking, daemon pushed its face close to mine and I smelled the stink of rotting meat emanating from its mouth. Then I saw another presence standing behind the daemon in my cell. Clad in a robe of fine linen with a shinning cloak wrapped about his shoulders I saw a face I had not seen in almost twenty years.

I looked past the daemon pressing in on me. "You cannot be here," I said. "How is this possible?"

He stood there smiling and said, "Of course I am here. It could be no other way."

"But you are dead."

"I am not dead."

He stood there calmly, radiating that self-assured manner of his. I reached out. He took my hand and pressed my palm against his cheek. "I am real. Feel my face. Look at me. I am as real as you."

He smiled at my surprise. "I have complete confidence in you," he told me. "You know what is right and you do the right things. Do not doubt yourself." And he was gone.

I saw a radiance of blue light emanating from the ceiling of my cell. I moved to stand under that light. I let it surround me. I said out loud, "In the light of grace I am." And then I repeated, "In the light of grace I am."

As I repeated my answer to the daemon's demand, it pulled back. Its bulging yellow eyes drew away from my face. I collapsed.

My brothers found me. And they brought me back.

At dinner some nights later they told me what they saw when they arrived. I lay outside my cell, and as they made their way up the hill toward me they feared they had come too late. But as they drew closer they saw I still breathed. So they picked me up and brought me inside the cave and lay me out on my robe. I stirred and spoke my uncle's name. They raised my head and held a flask of water to my lips.

> *"Blessed are the solitary and elect, for you will find the Kingdom. For you are from it, and to it you will return." Saying #49*

Grace and Redemption

Only self-awareness can bring forth the light of grace. Neither good works, nor fine words alone, nor faith nor forgiveness is enough. Forgiveness is an opening; it is the opening of the wound, and faith can provide courage to enter the wound. But through the wound must first come self-awareness before the light of grace can emerge. Grace is the light unto the world that shines through those who become aware.

> *His disciples said to Him, "Show us the place where You are, since it is necessary for us to seek it."*
>
> *He said to them, "Whoever has ears, let him hear. There is light within a man of light, and he lights up the whole world. If he does not shine, he is darkness." Saying #24*

The desert fathers did much to educate me. I saw how a community can create a good life from seemingly nothing. The very existence of this community in this place was a statement of proof for the parable of the fishes and the loaves in the Sermon on the Mount. There is always enough for all when all share what they have and support each other in a common quest.

In this barren place, we found unity of purpose that enabled our good works to provide us ample sustenance. And we found the solitude that gave us the self-awareness to hear and receive the wisdom that guided our good works.

I saw then that in movement and repose guided by the light of grace, I could find the release I sought from my burden of shame.

> *"If they say to you, 'Where did you come from?' say to them, 'We came from the light, the place where the light came into being on its own accord and established itself and became manifest through their image.'*
>
> *If they say to you, 'Is it you?' say, 'We are its children, we are the elect of the Living Father.'*
>
> *If they ask you, 'What is the sign of your father in you?' say to them, 'It is movement and repose.'" Saying #50*

Chapter 3

Servant Leader

In contrast to the obvious disintegration of the imperial government, the personal courage of the Christian martyrs was in itself impressive and persuasive. During times of public emergency, the Christians were often the only ones able to look after their members, bury their dead, and organize food supplies for the rest. Plainly, to be a Christian now brought more protection for the common person than to be a Roman. Leptis was not the only city that turned to the church. Where imperial officials could no longer be trusted or no longer cared, the church stepped in to fill the need.

In 386 I took up again my duties as bishop, but on the condition that while I would speak in Christian parables and theology during my sermons, I would remain free to think as a philosopher in my private life. Indeed it is precisely the merging of that duality created by the man of faith and the man of reason, the holy man and the philosopher, which encompasses the entirety of the question that each is trying to answer.

This year of 388 has been a good year. I am renewed and look forward to what each day offers with an energy and interest I have not felt in many years. My work has taken a new direction since my time in the desert, since release from my shame.

I resist giving people ready made answers to their questions. Instead I insist on thrashing out questions in public. I take the role of mediator and questioner of common assumptions, and refrain from too much preaching. The lively dialog that results is far more enlightening than any sermon I could deliver on my own. The consensus that emerges builds community far more strongly than any interpretations I alone might provide.

Religion is often controlled by those who act from the third motive while they attempt to convince others their actions come instead from the second motive. And religion is often taken up most passionately by those believers who act from the first motive. Yet enlightenment comes only to those genuinely animated by the second motive, those who are able to discern truth from lies, and who employ their strong belief to go beyond minutia and literal interpretations.

I reserve always my right to question. The meaning of some of the 114 sayings eludes me still, and I think often about what those sayings might mean. And there is one saying in particular that I believe I do understand, but with which I do not agree. To question is my duty and my place as a philosopher. How could I truly be a holy man if I were to blindly follow whatever has been written?

Religion and Literal Belief

Literal belief in the meaning of words and symbols has accompanied every religion since religion began. There is a story in our family that comes from the height of the Antonine Age, that age of peace and prosperity ushered in by the Pax Romana. There was a scandal then involving the priests of Jupiter and the wives of noble families. It was a time of easy prosperity, and it was easy to believe literally in the traditional religious myths.

Jupiter and Hercules were the patron gods of Leptis. The best families supplied the priesthoods for those gods, and the temple of Jupiter was the most marvelous of all the temples facing the old forum. One of my ancestors was the senior priest of Jupiter. Pious ladies of quality whose husbands wished for handsome and virile sons often prayed at the temple. It was said that Jupiter himself sometimes animated his statue in the temple and when he did, he answered the requests those who prayed to him. This was a literal belief professed by many at the time.

In reality it was the priests themselves who animated the cleverly designed statue of Jupiter. These priests spoke to their followers from the third motive. They had schemes for big benefits, and they scandalously abused the confidence of literal believers to convince them their messages were from the god himself. Unsuspecting husbands made generous donations to procure their devout wives the opportunity to pray alone in the temple on auspicious nights. And on those nights Jupiter would animate his statue and converse with these high born ladies.

This worked well for some years until one night the scandal was revealed by a priest who could not disguise the tone of his voice, and as the story goes in our family, "gave himself away in a moment of transport."

Another family story occurs during the Severan dynasty. Severus was deified by the Senate in Rome upon his death, and when this happened it meant, in the literal Roman way of thinking, that the family of Severus and their descendents were therefore gods themselves in some respects. The Punic traditions in our family and in many other fine families of Leptis created in us an instinctive attraction to this literal Roman definition of the divine.

Punic traditions run all the way back to the founding of Leptis and our family by a Phoenician merchant prince. Those traditions come from the practical experiences of a society focused intently on buying and selling and the accumulation of wealth. In such a world people rightly noted that success came from literal measures of value; from a reputation for goods that weighed exactly the stated amount; merchandise that was pure and unadulterated; products that were built well to meet high expectations.

Yet we forget that the ways of success in business are not necessarily the ways of success in other realms. The merchant cannot simply buy the approval of God as he would that of a customer. In Leptis on the piazza in front of the Baths of Hadrian there is a prominent example of this literal attempt to succeed in religion as one would succeed in business.

Facing the piazza across from the Nymphaeum is an exedra, a semi-circular colonnade made of fine Egyptian granite providing shade and shelter for people to sit and talk as they watch the flow of traffic and passersby. In this exedra is housed a fine statue dedicated to a daughter of Severus. Because Severus had been deified, his daughter was therefore also a goddess of some standing. The mantle of state religion at that time ennobled the living presence of our family.

In his zeal to reap the benefits of this official family religion, the donor of the exedra and statue, who was himself a nephew of Severus, tried earnestly to speak to his fellow citizens from the second motive; he strove to show them the strength of his religious belief. His words however, gave him away as one who actually spoke from the third motive; the one driven consciously or unconsciously by schemes for gain. He was not as successful as the priests of Jupiter because the good times of the Antonine Age were by then more a memory than a reality. And this made people less quick to embrace scheming stories than had once been the case. Yet my ancestor made a strong pitch nonetheless. His inscription on the pedestal supporting the statue proclaims the following:

To Septimia Polla, daughter of
Lucius Septimius Severus, duumvir, forever priest,
has Publius Septimius Geta, heir of his most sacred sister,
erected this statue from 144½ pounds of silver
and 10½ ounces of the most splendid quality, as decreed in her will.
To this gift was added in addition, 4½ pounds,
10½ ounces of silver more than had been bequeathed.

To the literal Punic mind this inscription could be seen as a sign of utmost religious devotion. In olden times we Phoenicians literally sacrificed our newborn children to show our total devotion to the supreme god Ba'al Hammon. Over time we made the transition to substituting first slaves and then money in the place of human flesh. It was certainly less harmful, but still every bit as sanctimonious and self-righteous in its ritual public display of seeking after personal aggrandizement.

My ancestor wanted to remind everyone that he too was descended from a divine family. And as a sign of his own divinity he quite literally fulfilled the family obligations and then exceeded those obligations by adding another measure of his own silver to the statue beyond what was called for in the contract. What more proof of divinity or at least divine favor did one need than that?

Religion to Divide or Unite

Literalism is not confined to pagans. It is both a source of pride and a source of suffering for the Christians. Literal interpretations have created much suffering because of fixation on minutia. This is a shame. If one is able to contemplate the higher meaning inherent in the words, it might be seen that different interpretations still point to the same meaning. There could be community instead of strife. Because of literalism, the Christians and the emperors first fought each other and then embraced each other.

As the empire slipped into chaos during the time of the military anarchy, there were periodic campaigns by generals who held the title of emperor who wished to strengthen their hold on power by requiring all citizens to swear an oath of allegiance. This required making an offering of wine or incense to the genus of the Roman Empire as symbolized by the statue of a deified emperor. Christians sometimes refused on principle to make such offerings to what they claimed was a false god, meaning literally the empire itself. That claim at times provoked an angry response from generals who were used to instant obedience, and who resorted to harsh punishment when faced with this defiance.

As the last great Christian persecutions under the Emperor Diocletian came to an end almost a hundred years ago, Bishop Donatus of Carthage declared those who had violated the prohibitions against worshiping a false god during that time could not be admitted back into the church until their last day in this mortal world, and even then, only if they had lived the remainder of their lives in strict adherence to the Christian rules and obligations.

In Africa the persecutions had been harsh, and many of the faithful had broken under the pressure. There were people who lit a stick of incense and repeated an oath of loyalty to the statue of an emperor in the city temple to avoid being fed to lions in the amphitheater. And there were clergy who turned over sacred books and silver chalices and candlestick holders from church alters into the impure hands of imperial officials.

> *They showed Jesus a gold coin and said to Him, "Caesar's men demand taxes from us."*
> *He said to them, "Give Caesar what belongs to Caesar, give God what belongs to God, and give Me what is Mine." Saying #100*

Then after Diocletian, starting with Emperor Constantine, the emperors turned to Christianity as a source of unity, and it became of the highest importance for all people to join or rejoin the church. Other bishops saw this and held that those who had fallen away could present petitions for forgiveness, and after doing appropriate, but not unreasonable acts of penance, they would be welcomed back into the community of the church. A most eloquent and persuasive spokesman for this point of view is Augustine, bishop of Hippo on the coast west of Carthage.

Yet to the literal mind, the Donatist position can be seen as the most righteous. However, this form of literal faith, while perhaps pure, is useless as a way to hold together a community or an empire. The mortal condition is inevitably one of error whether conscious or unconscious, and if religion only condemns and does not forgive, then it separates instead of unites. It forces believers to lie and hide their own transgressions, and it forces them to selectively overlook the actions of other believers in order to preserve community with them. This undermines community itself.

The Donatists felt the less demanding terms of penance offered to the fallen by the Orthodox Church made a mockery of their cherished notions of suffering and devotion to Christian ideals. In refutation of their position, Bishop Augustine issued many finely reasoned treatises and debated in Carthage with those adhering to the Donatist position. Augustine triumphed in those debates, yet few minds were changed.

The followers of Donatus are by this time several generations removed from those Christians who actually faced and suffered the imperial persecutions, but they nonetheless cling stubbornly to the literal interpretations of their now deceased bishop. And because their eternal souls are at stake, the stakes are too high for them to make any compromise whatsoever.

I have resolved to avoid the trap of literal interpretations. Too frequently, it makes people into fools or martyrs. And I have no use for either.

Family and Fortune

Many days I plan my activity so as to take me past the Arch of Severus at some point on my rounds. The arch is the symbol of Leptis; it is the monument people in other cities think of when one mentions our city. It stands where the two main thoroughfares come together. It is where the coast road, which becomes the decumanus once inside the city walls, crosses the road from the countryside to the south, which inside the walls becomes the cardo. These two busy streets provide the setting for the arch. Standing in the middle of the traffic circle where they connect, the arch is raised on a platform several steps above the roadway, and its thick pillars and heavy masonry presence provide cool shade for one like me to stand and watch the goings on.

Looking down the cardo toward the sea reminds me once more that Leptis is still a great city. There is a comforting bustle of carts going past and people walking by on their way to someplace. It is home yet for 40,000 souls, maybe more. The walls are still strong and well defended, even if the countryside becomes less secure.

My family and its fortunes are inseparably tied up with Leptis. We are the Septimiani. An illustrious ancestor of mine is said to be the one who stood up in the city council and demanded that the city add the superlative "Magna" to its name so as to distinguish us from that other Leptis, that little fishing village further up the coast to the west on the way to Carthage.

After general acclaim, this ancestor led a delegation of our finest families to Rome where a petition was filed with the Senate. Business arrangements were discussed with influential families there. Receptions were held, parties were given, and negotiations continued on through the summer. And then in the fall of that year, as the wheat and the olives were being harvested on our estates, word reached us. A proclamation had been issued by the Senate in Rome. We and our city would then, and forever more be known as Leptis Magna – Leptis the Great.

On summer mornings when I can, I rise before dawn and make my way through the sleeping city, down cobbled streets past quietly bubbling fountains to the old forum by the sea. There I take my place on a long curving white marble bench donated by my great, great, great uncle many years ago specifically for the enjoyment of this daily event. This event is as entertaining to me as any theater performance, as uplifting as any church service, and gives me as much wisdom as any holy man or soothsayer.

As I watch in the darkness, first there comes a morning glow that starts in the eastern sky. All is still and quiet; the waves on the seawall are the only sound. On my left, facing the forum are the imposing, classical city temples dedicated to Jupiter and the Antonine Age. On my right is the city senate house where the judges and magistrates used to meet before the Severan Basilica was built. In front of me, across the forum, are the seawall and the sea beyond.

The sky gets lighter. On clear summer days the sun rises in majesty like silent thunder across the harbor. It is framed by the towering lighthouse at the harbor entrance and the limestone warehouses that line the quay. As the sun continues its rise, I feel the city wake up. By the time the sun has reached the top of the lighthouse, the city has gone from quiet and expectant to a swelling clatter of familiar sounds.

And while this scene is unfolding, insights come to me. I see how this or that problem or opportunity can be addressed. Profoundly obvious ideas that I had not seen before appear in my mind bearing useful answers to nagging questions. This early morning practice of movement and repose has proven time and again to be one of my best sources of advice. And there is another source of advice I depend upon as well.

Seeing with Both Eyes

We are given two eyes because we need both the left eye and the right eye to see the world in all its dimensions. Seeing with one eye alone gives us a flat picture lacking in depth. It is not that one eye is better than the other; it is simply that we need the perspective of both eyes to see the world clearly.

One could also say this is an allegory for needing both the male and the female. One is not superior to the other; it is simply that they are the duality which defines the whole. I have found it is best to have the female in my life even though I am the bishop and I am expected to be chaste. That is a case of literalism again taken too far. I will not flaunt this convention in public, but neither will I endure this prohibition in private.

Behind the literalism there is also a pragmatic consideration. I am father of the community and must rise above my own family to earnestly embrace all members of the community. Therefore, like the good emperors of the Antonine Age, it is proper and desirable that I have no children of my own so as not to be tempted to favor them above all others, and by so doing bring harm to the community. It follows then that I should not marry if I am not to father children and produce heirs. This I understand and accept.

After returning from my time with the desert fathers, I met a woman. I have known her now for many years. She was the widow of a noble husband killed in the raids. We met over dinner at the house of a cousin who told me later she could not resist the chance to bring two such kindred souls together. This woman was familiar. She had a dramatic flair, and I knew her from somewhere before. We chatted across the table and I felt her gaze, "You interest me. Pay attention to me!" I could not resist.

Walking home that night I suddenly realized she was the woman I saw at the city gate on the second day of the raids so many years ago. She stood atop the city wall pleading for her husband's life with the tribesmen below who held him captive. She gave away her gold and jewelry to ransom him. What else could she do? And when they turned him loose, and he was hoisted up to the top of the walls, we all saw the extent of his injuries. We knew he would not live beyond another two days.

After the raids she moved, as many did, from her country estate to the protection of the city. She took up residence in her grandfather's house.

It was only a few blocks from my own. It was even closer to the shore and the sound of the sea.

She was a pious lady of impeccable upbringing. As we got to know each other in the years that followed, we found we enjoyed the companionship more and more. She had the ability to speak truth to power. She could tell me things about a person at a glance, things that would take me forever to see or not at all. I fancied I was able to do something similar for her when it came to more abstract matters.

Her habit of speaking truth did not come without friction. There were times when I had enough of truth. The recitation of my admitted faults did not make them disappear any faster. There were times when I resolved to see her no more, and forced my mind to turn to other things. Those were not productive times, and thankfully in the few instances when I did turn away from her, she responded by turning toward me.

There have been days when the pleasure of her company while sitting in the garden, walking down a street, or eating our dinner together has been sublime.

> *"If two make peace with each other in this one house, they will say to the mountain, 'Move Away,' and it will move away." Saying #48*

I was often invited to dine with her and her grandfather and their other guests. It became my habit and privilege to stay quietly as her grandfather retired, and other guests bid good night.

There have been nights when the rhythm of the waves merged with the scent of incense and the sound of chimes in the garden. In those times I experienced the duality of the priest standing before the alter, the duality of the worshiper and the object of worship. And when these two merge, the bliss that follows is both movement and repose.

Turning of the Wheel

FORTUNAE VOLUCRIS ROTA, ADVERSA PROSPERIS SEMPER ALTERNANS.

Fortune's rapid wheel, is always interchanging adversity and prosperity.

In this year of 394 the empire still provides us with reason to exist. The empire provides markets for our oil. Despite the ravages of raids, the green sea of olive trees still produces enormous quantities of oil. Our lives are measured in the yearly cycle of pruning the trees, tending them, harvesting them and pressing the olives for their oil. Behind this most visible cycle is the other cycle of storing the oil, selling the oil and transporting the oil. These two cycles combine to provide the heartbeat that keeps the city alive.

It is my place to call forth common purpose to unite us and renew our courage in face of the challenges that confront us. In this world Leptis is only one actor in a play containing many new actors. I spend much of my time defining and promoting stories and themes for this play. I make the theme noble and uplifting because people long to commit to something noble, even those who say they do not. I give the story many good roles, not just a few leading roles, otherwise there is no inducement for the many actors to learn their lines.

I do not huddle behind city walls. I meddle in everything. It seems there is a need for someone to play this meddling role and I have become well suited to it. The role itself calls for exercise of qualities I have worked long to develop. Often I find the possibilities in situations that no one else sees. Often I see the truth and recognize the lies. The more I exercise these skills the more reliable they become.

I look for ways to guide the ambitions and desires of the desert tribes and the farmer soldiers into results that benefit the city as well as themselves. I spend time with the farmer soldiers in their fortified communities and desert valleys. When tribal chiefs come to meet the farmer clans, often I am there. I am there to find what we have in common and find ways to strengthen those bonds. If I cannot depend on force to protect me, then I must turn to persuasion. And persuasion works best when I offer people something they want, and then show them how to get it.

The farmer soldiers know the harbor of Leptis is the shipping point for their crops and the point of entry for the gold coins and luxury goods they acquire from us in exchange. The desert tribes know they need us to buy the ivory and ebony slaves and wild animals that come on caravans through their desert. They understand how each can benefit.

But on another level they hate us. And we in turn hate them. Respect and trust easily give way to greed and fear. Each imagines they can prosper without the other. There is always a delicate balance that must be found and it is ever shifting because the stories and traditions we have in common have become so tenuous.

In the empire there is no longer a single power that can rule over all. There is the emperor, and the army, and the church, and the noble families. The empire itself is divided into the western empire and the eastern empire. There is no "captain of all captains," as the soldiers say in their broken Latin. It is the strength we find in communities of our own making that provides for our survival. And those things we share in common determine how far that strength can take us.

Techniques of Prophesy

On my Punic side I believe I have never really shed my deepest inner belief that worship is primarily just ritualized appeasement of divine wrath. And I see that particular belief resonates with many others as well – people of Leptis, desert farmers and people of the desert tribes.

People are forever looking for the right words and the right sequence of steps to create the rituals that best accomplish this appeasement. So at times I give them what they are looking for. When Horatio stood alone on the bridge, he had to enhance his strength and the effect of his arms. He could not hope to fend off his attackers by physical strength alone. So he found ways to keep them off balance, to make them confused and hesitant. As bishop of Leptis I do the same to defend our bridge.

It is most useful to be seen as a divinely possessed holy man when I have to face down an ambitious and greedy desert chief. I combine the symbols of regency, which this chief often eagerly wants, with trappings of magic and sorcery. They believe me to be half mad with supernatural powers of prophecy, and sometimes there is reason to think this might be true, at least in part. At times I see trajectories of people and events that accurately predict where they will be in a moment or a month or a year, an "astute sense of the obvious" someone once called it. Yet often enough what is obvious to me is missed completely by those around me.

I give the tribes reason to fear my prophecy by shamelessly confusing them as to cause and effect. I have spoken from the third motive, told big lies to gain big benefits while carefully concealing it from those I lied to. I have used my astute sense of the obvious to pretend it was me who caused what I could only predict. I turned to this use of prophecy out of desperation at a time when I had nothing to loose and no escape. And to my amazement, it worked.

Since my time with the desert fathers I am able to recognize well enough what is most probably true and what is most probably false. This self-knowledge and insight has guided my actions in moments of dire need. My normally cautious and sensitive nature would never have permitted me to take such risks before my time in the desert.

On returning to Leptis from Skete, I found the tribes aggressive and the farmer soldiers indifferent. Something had to be done. There was the press of unrelenting necessity, the fire at my back, and there was only one way forward. I took a dangerous path, as I had when I confronted my daemon in the desert. In council with the farmers and the desert chiefs on night, I stood and raised my arms to pray not knowing what I would say. In the silence of that moment when all eyes were upon me, I heard the Muse whisper in my ear. I repeated aloud what I heard her say and walked away. When those predictions soon came true, I took full credit for causing them to happen.

After the miracle of those first predictions, my reputation was established. My prophesies do not always come true, but often they do come true or partly true, and people forget the ones that do not come true. They want to forget them. They want to believe I am possessed of supernatural powers. Whether they fear me or praise me, it is important to them to have a wizard or a holy man in their lives. It validates their important beliefs about how the world works, and I am, for the most part, glad to oblige them.

In the midst of difficult negotiations or tense situations, I fix my opponents with a steady gaze. I recite words of wisdom in a language they barely understand, in a voice that is clear and strong. And when I have their full attention I make a dramatic gesture to drive home my point. I step forward suddenly, and they shrink back. I raise my arms to invoke the Almighty, and they bow their heads. Then I turn and walk away while they stand rooted to the spot in silence and awe.

I combine rhetorical techniques with an ability to recognize truth. Imperious behavior and unpredictable actions taken with great conviction serve to keep opponents on their guard and nervous about provoking one such as myself, one who seems to have the power to commune with daemons and angels and even the Almighty. I bestow symbols of regency on one chief knowing it will induce him to suppress the ambitions of a rival chief. I pronounce dire prophecy on others when I see them headed for obvious trouble, and then take credit as the magical source of their misfortunes when those misfortunes occur.

From Jovinus I learned well the business of wheat and oil, well enough to show the soldier farmers good reasons to defend the desert watering places and use their influence to discourage the tribes from raiding our coastal estates and city. They do this to protect their own lucrative trade with us. It is a delicate balance based on traditions and pragmatic procedures that I discover to be effective. I am sometimes surprised at the things I do.

I can only hope my example will, like the example of the five good emperors, be followed by those who come after me, at least for a time. If this were to happen it could, I think, create a golden age in this later empire. That is what I tell myself. The alternative, the failure to find ways to guide the strivings of powerful people, will lead to a cycle of disintegration which I cannot bear to imagine.

Allegory for the Present

Tonight I open the shutters of my library windows and look out over a city under a full moon. It is a picture painted in a soft light in shades of white, grey and black punctuated here and there by open windows giving out a faint yellow glow from candles and lamps. I hear the sound of waves and I smell the ocean just a short walk down the street from my front door. I place the candles and olive oil lamps in my library to create a circle of light.

I write these words in the year of our Lord 412 in the reign of the Emperor Honorius, ruler of the western empire. We are caught up in cycles of misfortune. For reasons that range from strong belief in things that are not true, to endless schemes for personal gain, we betray the principles we profess to believe in. These betrayals destroy the things we have in common, so their loss drives us into smaller communities and less connected worlds. The common good is sacrificed for the momentary interests of a few.

We long for those days gone by that we are told were a Golden Age. Yet the only age we ever have is this age. There is no going back. We do not get younger. Time seems to flow inexorably in one direction. So what then is history if not an allegory for the present? It is a guide for what we can do today based upon the lessons we learn from observing the past. The only age that can ever be a golden age is this age. If this age cannot be a golden age then golden ages cannot exist.

I learn every day my immortality is not a personal achievement, it is a communal achievement. Every person inevitably will die. Every person will give up everything they own, or have it taken from them. But our collective presence does not die. One could say our collective presence is embodied in the city and in our stories of the city.

We seek immortality, and yet miss the vessel of our immortality which is standing right in front of us. The city is us for a while and then it passes on to others. For that time we give life to the city, the meaning of our lives comes from doing what we do to perpetuate and strengthen the city. The city is the community that receives us back into its embrace when we emerge on the other side. That is the immortality we seek.

Yet Leptis grows weaker along with the empire that provides our reason to exist. Our world slips out of control in spite of vigorous efforts to prevent this from happening. Our efforts do not deliver the results we seek, yet we seem powerless to change. In striving to protect our wealth we hoard it, and in the act of hoarding, it disappears. We attempt to grow food while neglecting the land on which the crops are planted, and then claim not to know why more and more go hungry. People's reasons to care are destroyed, and their ability to speak is lost. Yet it need not be so. This cycle is not preordained.

It is said that, "History does not repeat itself; people repeat history because they learn nothing from it."

At times, in the face of this relentless and seemingly futile repetition of history, I shift my attention away from the minutia around me and focus on the universal life that throbs within us all. We have free will; never is an undertaking impossible. The light of grace is always present.

> *"I am the light that shines over all things. I am everything. From me all came forth, and to me all return. Split a piece of wood, and I am there. Lift a stone, and you will find me there."* Saying #77

When my day arrives for the victory of death, death will close in but it will not triumph. I celebrate life's enduring victory in the very kiss of my own annihilation. There are days when I strain to hear the shout from the opposite bank.

Chapter 4

Currents of History

There are places where something happened that needs to be remembered. Places where history speaks from the stones, the earth, the wind itself. Those places speak and we cannot help but listen; something resonates within us and we feel compelled to understand its meaning. We cannot get it out of our minds until its truths become clear. Such a place has haunted me for many years.

I came across Leptis Magna when I was a boy of eight years old in the year 1961. My family lived in Tripoli, Libya. My father worked for a company exploring for oil in the Sahara desert. East of Tripoli about a two hour drive along the coast road was the ruins of an ancient Roman city where the desert comes down close to the shore of the Mediterranean Sea.

One cool autumn day we took a drive down the coast road to explore that ancient city. When we got there we turned off the paved road and rolled slowly over a gravel road to a wide, sandy parking lot where we parked the car and got out. There were a couple of other cars there but nobody else in sight. The smell of the sea was in the air, and I could hear the sound of waves in the distance. A breeze blew off the water and the sky formed a backdrop of low hanging gray clouds with occasional bright patches where sunlight shone through.

Place Where a Presence Lingers

As we entered the city, walls rose up here and there from the weeds and the rubble on either side of a flagstone paved road. Groups of stone pillars stood out in the distance, and the remains of houses and shops and monumental buildings were everywhere.

"Dad" I asked, "where did everybody go?" It was inconceivable to me that such a big city as this had once obviously been could now be abandoned. What happened to all the people who lived here? Why did they leave? How could that have happened? I wanted to know.

I don't remember what my father said in response, but as we walked, I sensed a presence. When I closed my eyes it was as if someone was whispering to me in a language I could almost understand, but not quite. I sensed the voice behind those words was trying to tell me something important. His presence seemed to radiate from the bricks and columns and cobblestones. Everywhere we went that day as we wandered through the ruins, he was there

We walked down broad avenues paved with carefully fitted flagstones worn smooth with use by people and wagons in a world from 1800 years ago. We walked through ruins of monumental buildings made of huge stone blocks and marble pillars and arches. Where the walls were gone, we could still see remains of mosaic floors made of carefully fitted pieces of different colored marble.

We came to a huge plaza, an open space surrounded by high walls and broken columns. At one end was the ruin of an enormous basilica; its brick walls still stood several stories high. This was the main public space of the city. We walked across it; it was littered with fragments of statues and broken pillars and stone faces with staring eyes. There were pedestals for statues now long gone; but which still displayed their inscriptions, etched in familiar letters spelling words I could almost understand.

We left this plaza through a tall stone gateway that looked out toward the sea. I remember walking down a street to the theater that must once have held audiences of thousands. I walked across the stage and looked up at the receding rows of stone seats. We climbed up those rows of seats until we got to the highest level, and sitting there with my father, I could see out over the marble columns set in the back of the stage wall. Off in the distance was the sea; a wind was blowing and there were whitecaps on the crests of the waves.

We followed another street to the harbor. It was all silted up. There was sand, tall grass and desert weeds where once water had been. Stone quays circled to the left and to the right around the sides of what had been a big round anchorage for ships. We walked across the dry ground of the harbor and out to the end of the quay where the foundations of the city lighthouse still stood. Big blocks of stone as tall as I was had once been used to build the tower of the lighthouse; now they were tumbled into the surf.

I stood there with the wind coming off the sea and the sound of the waves surging onto the rocks, and looked back across the ruins of the city. I could feel a sense of greatness turned to ruin, a deep, aching sadness. It was by then late in the afternoon; the yellow-orange light of the setting sun was breaking through the clouds in places. The ruins cast long shadows. Except for the six of us, there was no one else around. And yet I knew someone else was there. All I had to do was close my eyes and listen, and over the sound of the waves I could hear a faint whispering.

We returned to Leptis several more times. And each time I felt that presence. I sensed it was a man who had lived there a very long time. He seemed part of the place. It seemed like he wanted to tell me something he thought was very important. What was it? I couldn't understand. He asked questions. It made me uncomfortable. What did he want?

I think I know now what it was he wanted from me. He heard the questions I asked my father as we walked through his city, and my questions were the same as his.

> *"The man old in days will not hesitate to ask a small child seven days old about the place of life, and he will live. For many who are first will become last, and they will become one and the same." Saying #4*

Paths that Cross Will Cross Again

When I was 10 we left Libya, and I hardly ever thought about Leptis after that. When I finished college I moved to a big American city on the coast of one of the Great Lakes. My house is downtown in a comfortable residential neighborhood of older two and three story brick and limestone buildings. It's located just a short walk from a beach on the shore of Lake Michigan. Often I find myself walking along the shore listening to the sound of the waves, and over the years, my thoughts have been drawn back time and again to that city by the sea on the edge of the Sahara desert.

Driven by an interest that grew into almost an obsession, I have looked for, and found, and read countless books, articles and archeological reports about his city, about his family, and about the period of history when he lived. He lived in a period of epic cultural change known to historians as Late Antiquity. This was a time when the classical world as it had existed since the early Greek city states such as Athens and Sparta passed away with the collapse of its last great civilization – the Roman Empire. And in its place, from the remnants of that dead world, its surviving citizens mixed with invading tribes and created the medieval world of kings and queens, knights and ladies, priests, peasants, merchants and wizards.

Over the years information about his city, his family and his period of history came to me in the form of old books found while wandering through used bookstores, pictures of Leptis taken by my parents on our visits there discovered inside an envelope in a family scrapbook, and countless articles and pictures that came to me while doing Internet searches on subjects I can no longer recall.

I got the impression more than once that this information found me, I didn't find it. When one of these finds caught my attention, I knew it was because it was part of a bigger picture. I studied it, and thought about what it meant, and how it might relate to other finds that had come to me.

The bigger picture has revealed itself to me bit by bit over many years. I have traveled down more paths, literally and figuratively, than I can count. I have explored this man who spoke to me at Leptis and his Late Roman world from dozens of perspectives and historical narratives. Over the years this information has seeped into my subconscious mind, which in its patient and mysterious way, has found areas of overlap in the different perspectives and narratives. It has used the multiple layers of data that those overlaps provide to create three-dimensional models or holograms of scenes and people. And sometimes, I find those scenes and people have even acquired the ability to move.

Understanding starts when I organize enough facts to form a plausible picture drawn like a mural or a comic strip on the wall of a long hallway. Yet this is still just a flat, two-dimensional rendering. Real insight happens as I move along this flat mural and suddenly am able to reach my arms into the picture and see the objects there in three dimensions. Then, in some of those three-dimensional places, I go even further, and the scene starts to move. It becomes a simulation; a holographic movie that shows what most likely happened in those scenes that it plays back for me. And in those three-dimensional places and holographic movies, there is a presence; someone emerges from the background and speaks to me.

Strivings of Powerful People

Ever since I saw the ruins of Leptis Magna when I was a boy, I've wondered about the fall of the Roman Empire. It has become one of the central allegories I use in making sense of the current world. The Roman world was a smaller world and maybe a simpler world, but still quite sophisticated and filled with people every bit as smart as we are, and as scheming and short-sighted as we are. And in that world there were people who thought great thoughts and did great things that affect us even now.

It always seemed so tragic and unnecessary. That fading of the light of learning, that forgetting of the knowledge and culture of the classical world, lost under an onslaught of invading tribes and crushing poverty and corrupt officials and repressive literal religions. Why did it happen? Could it have been avoided?

Over the years, I've come to see that it did not have to happen, but it became inevitable. People were aware their eternal empire was falling apart, but were unable to do anything to prevent its collapse. That civilization was unable to constructively channel the strivings of the powerful people who tore it apart. Any civilization, whether that of the Roman Empire or that of our world today, exists first and foremost to channel the strivings of powerful people into socially constructive ends. When a civilization no longer performs that function, it must, and will, die.

Leptis Magna is a lense through which I see a period in history when one world died and another world emerged. It provides stories and allegories that I use to ponder similar events happening in the world today.

Those events are driven by questions about the relationship between personal success and the success of our wider society. What is good for me and my family? And what is good for our city, our country, our world? Our answers to these questions speak directly to the things we are willing to do in order to get what we want.

What Became of Leptis

Leptis was irrevocably caught up in the decline of the empire that gave it reason to exist. As the empire collapsed, Leptis faded away.

In 429 there came the arrival of another tribe to Africa. This time it was a Germanic tribe, the Vandals. In the bitterly cold winter of the year 406, that tribe and other northern tribes had gathered on the far side of the Rhine. There were no longer enough Roman soldiers to hold them back, so the warriors accompanied by their families and livestock and wagons walked across the frozen river. They wandered, raiding and pillaging through the remnants of the Roman provinces now known as France and Spain. At the straits of Gibraltar they crossed over to Africa. It is said by some that they were invited into Africa by the Roman general there, Count Boniface, to help him in a rebellion against the western emperor. In any case, once in Africa, the Vandals defeated that general and became the rulers themselves.

They captured Carthage and the other Roman cities of Africa and tore down the walls of those cities to prevent them from rebelling. In Leptis the desert began to invade even the heart of the city. The new rulers did little to defend the city. Without its walls Leptis was lost, and when the desert tribes came again, the city was burned and largely abandoned. A hundred years later in 533 the Vandals were in turn defeated by the eastern emperor Justinian who sent his army to reconquer North Africa. Leptis became a small coastal outpost for the eastern empire by then known as the Byzantine Empire.

The Byzantines built new walls around an even smaller area of Leptis. They restored the Severan basilica and christened it the "Church of the Mother of God." A hundred years after that in 643, the Arab armies of Islam swept up out of Arabia and across North Africa. The Byzantines defending the province of Tripolitania were defeated, and Leptis was left to be buried by the desert sands. Its very name was forgotten.

The Green Sea of olive trees and the fertile desert valleys exist today only in isolated pockets. Their reason for being withered away as the rest of the empire disappeared. The elaborate network of dams and underground cisterns and irrigation channels that carefully captured and stored and distributed the precious rainwater fell into disrepair. There was no demand for the crops that the network grew, and there were no people who remembered how to keep the network in good repair.

Huge stone piers for olive presses from 1600 years ago stand scattered across hillsides and ravines deep in the desert like silent doorways into another time. When these stone piers were rediscovered by Europeans, they were assumed to be Paleolithic monuments such as those at Stonehenge. For what other reason would people build such massive structures on rocky hillsides out in the desert? They could not imagine these hillsides and plains had once been covered by forests of olive trees and dotted with farm houses and wheat fields.

There were many possible outcomes that could have evolved. There were many ways for the Romans, the farmers, the tribes and the invading Vandals and Arabs to mix and combine. Nothing was preordained. Yet only those combinations that could channel the strivings of powerful people into constructive ends had any chance of lasting. What happened in Leptis is an example of this law in action.

Illusion of Time

Lately, in the middle of traffic or as I walk down a crowded city street, it is as if someone's memories come back to me in flashes. I feel a shudder go through me, my breath catches in my throat, memories wash over me and I am often brought to the verge of tears. I hear his thoughts. And my eyes glimpse scenes from a long time ago.

It happens especially on windy, overcast days when grey clouds hang low on the horizon and I am near the water and the sound of waves washing up on a beach or breaking against a seawall. I feel his presence.

I am starting to understand this man and his story. I walked the streets of his city. I stood in the same spaces where he stood. I touched the same marble columns he touched. I asked the same questions he asked. I realize what he wants is for me to tell his story.

There are many nights when I wake after only a few hours of sleep and put on my robe and go into my study and turn on my desk lamp and open my web browser. Then in the light of my softly glowing computer screen, I pick up where I left off the night before.

There is something about the accumulation of pictures and text and the interconnections that grow between related clusters of information in that spreading planetary cerebral cortex we call the Internet. Perhaps I and billions of others like me are nerve cells in a larger mind that is becoming aware of itself.

Connections form between related facts, and as more connections are made, even more connections are made. A threshold is reached. Memories from a long time ago reform and come alive again because the presence that exists in those memories awakens and reaches out to those who can hear it.

One night I came upon a website devoted to the work of another African bishop, Bishop Augustine of Hippo, now known as Saint Augustine. He and Lucius were contemporaries; they were both bishops of important cities in Roman Africa. I'm certain they knew each other personally and shared beliefs in common. Regarding time, Augustine had this to say, and I'm sure Lucius would agree:

> *"I have therefore come to the conclusion that time is nothing other than tension: but tension of what I do not know, and I would be*

very surprised if it is not the tension of consciousness itself."
St. Augustine, *The Confessions*

On these nights the hours go by quickly. The sky outside my study windows starts to brighten. I realize he has kept me up all night once again, researching his stories and connecting his memories. I hear his voice and I write down his words. And I ask once more, "Why me?"

I always get the same answer; he tells me he talks to me because I can hear him. He says he must tell me these stories because stories heard only by the dead are stories lost to oblivion. Though Leptis is now in ruins, the city did not die. Its people fought the good fight, they said their prayers and dove into the river to return to the other side where they live still in this city on the edge of the desert.

Leptis is a bridge to another time.

Stand at the end of the harbor breakwater on a late fall day when the setting sun breaks through the clouds in patches of reddish orange light that skims across the wave tops. Feel the cold west wind and its message of approaching winter. ∞

Postscript

Timeless Theme

Years ago I came across an envelope in a family photo album and inside it were pictures my mother took of us on our first trip to Leptis. There is my father investigating the ruins of the Severan Basilica. There is my father and me and my sister looking out over the theater, and that's us climbing over broken pillars lining one of the quays of the silted up harbor. The last photo shows my two brothers and my sister posed for a picture. Looking at it, I suddenly saw myself in the lower right foreground, eyes closed, listening to something.

Soon after finding these pictures I came upon the works of the Roman historian Ammianus Marcellinus. He served several emperors and traveled widely. His work is a primary source for much of what is known about events in the Later Roman Empire, that period historians call Late Antiquity.

One of his books tells about what happened in Leptis Magna during and after the raids in 363 and 364. He tells of Jovinus, Count Romanus, Remegius, Palladius and the Emperor Valentinian. He describes how Leptis sent a delegation to appeal to the emperor for protection, and how Romanus tricked Palladius, and bribed the magistrates of Leptis, and arranged for Jovinus to be tried and executed for lying to the emperor. I knew then this was the story Lucius wanted to tell me, and wanted me to tell others.

Ammianus Marcellinus provided the dates and the names and events. Septimius Lucius gave me the telling details, and told me of the emotions and fears that drove the people.

Lucius also pushed me to discover, to read and to think about the Gospel of Thomas. I am not a religious person, and I fancy I can tell the difference between glib nonsense and real wisdom. I am not interested in theological debates nor religious dogma, and resisted looking into this gospel even as it kept coming up again and again. I realize now those sayings spoken with their simple, blunt truth are the only way for Lucius, and for me, to come to terms with this story, and make peace with what happened at Leptis Magna.

Ammianus Marcellinus Vol. III, Ammianus Marcellinus, John C. Rolfe, translator, Cambridge MA, London UK: The Loeb Classical Library, 1939, Book XXVIII, 6

The Gospel of Thomas, Commentary & Typing by Craig Schenk, Translations by: Thomas O. Lambdin (Coptic version); B.P Grenfell & A.S. Hunt (Greek Fragments); Bentley Layton (Greek Fragments), 6/17/92, Made available to the net by Paul Halsall (halsall@murray.fordham.edu), http://www.sacred-texts.com/chr/thomas.htm

Grand Promenade and Lighthouse of Leptis

PIE IESU
QUI TOLLIS PECCATA MUNDI
DONA EIS REQUIEM

Printed in Great Britain
by Amazon

83131730R10119